Now that I've gotten to know you better, I suppose I can comfortably spend the night with you."

Logan took her hand and helped her to her feet. "Since I've been instructed by my brother to keep an eye on you, you can have the sofa and I'll sleep in the lounger."

"You really don't have to do that. I'm feeling fine." Not exactly true. Knowing he was so close made her a little lightheaded.

"Look, Jenna, unless you're going to trust me enough to sleep in the same bed with you, you're going to have to deal with me staying in the living room so I can watch you."

She wasn't certain she could trust *herself* to sleep in the same bed with him. "Okay, but you don't have to watch me all night."

He ran a fingertip along her cheek. "I have no problem watching you all night."

1

Dear Reader,

I'm absolutely thrilled and honored to see the release of my first Special Edition book! This particular story features Logan O'Brien, another of the O'Brien family siblings previously introduced in Silhouette Desire. *Through Jenna's Eyes* explores the challenges a visually impaired single mom faces on a daily basis, and her chance meeting with a man stung by betrayal and lacking in trust. She soon sees beyond his steel facade to uncover the honorable man beneath, while he begins to view the world in a whole new light through his connection with her.

I have to admit, I had a wonderful time with Jenna and Logan's relationship. The definition of fire and ice, Jenna and Logan discover an incredible passion with each other that eventually leads to love. Most important, during the creation of this story, I relied on my experiences with friends and relatives who've faced failing vision with grace and dignity. They have served not only as my inspiration for Jenna, but as a reminder that the ability to see should never be taken for granted.

I hope you enjoy Logan and Jenna's journey as much as I've enjoyed writing it!

Happy reading!

Kristi

THROUGH
JENNA'S EYES

KRISTI GOLD

S PECIAL EDITION

Published by Silhouette Books

America's Publisher of Contemporary Romance

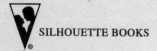

SILHOUETTE BOOKS

ISBN-13: 978-0-373-24836-0
ISBN-10:   0-373-24836-9

THROUGH JENNA'S EYES

KRISTI GOLD

admits to having a fondness for watching major league baseball and double-cheese enchiladas and she also enjoys creating dark and somewhat dangerous—albeit honorable—heroes. She considers indulging in all three in the same day as the next best thing to a beach vacation!

Kristi resides in central Texas with her retired physician husband and the occasional guest in the form of one of her three grown children. She loves to hear from readers, and can be contacted through her Web site at www.kristigold.com or through snail mail at 6902 Woodway Drive, #166, Waco, TX 76712. (Please include a SASE for response.)

To my daughter, Kendall Paige, for growing from a precious child into a remarkable young woman.

Chapter One

Logan O'Brien had learned long ago the phone always rang at inopportune times. During a shower, which he'd already taken. During sex, which unfortunately wasn't an issue tonight. And in this case, during an extra-inning ball game, which ranked right up there as another worst-case scenario.

After pausing the game with the remote, he grabbed the phone and answered with an irritable, "Yeah."

"Sorry to bother you, boss, but we have a situation."

Good old Bob, Logan's right-hand man. Whenever a problem arose, the retired cop always sounded as if he worked for a Secret Service detail, not as a driver for well-heeled Houston society. "It's late, Bob. I've got the ball game on and I've only been home for an hour. So, unless you're going to tell me that every limo or sedan I own has simultaneously broken down, you handle it."

"We've got an alleged intoxicated female who needs a ride."

Not the first time one of his employees had faced that situation. "And this is supposed to impress me how?"

"It's Jenna Fordyce."

Great. The daughter of his VIP client, Avery Fordyce. Logan's company took care of all the billionaire's corporate and personal transportation needs, not to mention the other clients Fordyce had sent his way. "What about Calvin?"

"He's off tonight. I'd do it, but I'm waiting to take a wedding party to the airport. And I thought since old man Fordyce trusts you, and this is—"

"I know, Bob. His kid." So much for a night of sitting around in his underwear, relaxing. "I'll take care of it. Where is she?"

"At a joint called La Danza. It's on—"

"I know the place." He'd been there before. Several times over the past year, but not in a few weeks. At least the nightclub was less than two miles from his downtown condo. But the Fordyce estate, where Jenna still resided, was located a good thirty minutes away, longer if the Saturday-night traffic happened to be heavy.

"The bouncer called dispatch about five minutes ago," Bob added. "He said he'd wait with her until someone got there. I'm thinking she's in pretty bad shape."

That didn't surprise Logan one bit. The club was known for its high-octane drinks. One or two martinis would do the trick for a lightweight socialite. "Fine. I'm on my way."

After hanging up the phone, Logan sprinted up the stairs to dress in a faded blue T-shirt, jeans and a pair of hiking boots, clothes he would never allow his employees to wear while conducting business. But if the heiress had tied one on, she probably wouldn't notice his attire. Even if she didn't approve, right now he only cared about getting this over with so he could get back to the game.

When he reached the parking garage, Logan opted to take his Hummer instead of the roadster, in case she happened to get sick. God, he hoped she didn't. That would pretty much ruin his night completely.

As he navigated the downtown streets, Logan realized he wasn't sure he'd be able to pick Jenna Fordyce out of a crowd, considering he'd never officially met her. But he had seen her framed high-school graduation photo on Avery's desk—a predictably beautiful, dark haired, dark eyed young woman. Daddy's little princess, just like Logan's ex-fiancée, who had played the pregnancy card until he'd called her bluff, fortunately before he'd been trumped into marriage.

Yeah, he'd had his fill of debutantes. Society babes who couldn't see beyond the fact he had the means and the money to keep them in the lifestyle to which they were accustomed. He doubted Jenna Fordyce was any different from the rest, particularly since she was the only child of a widowed business magnate.

A few minutes later, Logan pulled behind a stretch limo, the only space available beneath the portico of the five-star hotel that housed the popular nightclub. He stepped out into the warm June night and immediately caught sight of a no-neck guy with a clean-shaven head standing a few feet away, his arm around a woman.

The closer he came to the couple, the more certain he became that he'd found Jenna Fordyce—a few years older than depicted in the photo, but still as striking. She was conservatively dressed in a blue sleeveless blouse, a white skirt cut right above the knee and low heels. Her brown hair curled past her shoulders and a pair of sunshades covered her eyes, indicating she'd moved past three to at least four sheets in the wind. She was also pressing a white cloth over her right eyebrow, and Logan wondered if she'd engaged in a catfight. That would definitely make the society page tomorrow.

As he approached the unlikely pair, Logan nodded at the presumed bouncer and addressed the woman at his side. "Ms. Fordyce?"

She inclined her head toward him. "Yes?"

"I'm Logan O'Brien, the owner of your father's transportation service."

When he offered his hand, she ignored the gesture, fumbled in the skirt's pocket and withdrew several bills that she pressed into the bouncer's palm. "This should take care of the bar tab, Johnny, with a little extra for your help. And, if you don't mind, could you tell my friend I'm leaving now? I wouldn't want her to worry."

"What does she look like?" Johnny asked.

"A pretty blonde," she said. "Her name is Candice and she's seated at the bar. I believe she's wearing pink. She always wears pink."

The bouncer regarded Logan, his arm still firmly around his charge. "Someone needs to check out the cut on her head. She had a pretty nasty fall, but she wouldn't let me call the paramedics."

Jenna waved her free hand in dismissal. "It's nothing."

When Logan noticed the red seeping through the cloth, he realized the injury could be serious. "Johnny's right. You're bleeding. You need a doctor."

"Can we discuss this in the car?" she asked.

No discussion required. She could argue all the way to the hospital, but he wasn't about to turn her loose without making sure she was okay. "Let's go."

The bouncer held out her arm to Logan. "She's kind of shaky, so you need to hang on to her."

Usually Logan wouldn't mind wrapping his arm around a sexy woman. But this blue-blooded babe didn't interest him—or shouldn't—for several reasons.

Logan circled his arm around her waist and braced her elbow with one hand. Slowly, he guided her to the SUV, noticing immediately that she was small, maybe five-two, a foot shorter than him. Definitely not his type. He preferred women with more substance, inside and out.

Once they reached the passenger side, Logan opened the door, helped her up into the seat and, in a show of benevolence, buckled her in. So far, so good. She hadn't taken another tumble on the way, even though he suspected she might have if he'd let her go, considering how carefully she'd measured her steps. Whatever she'd had to drink, he assumed it must have been fairly potent. But he didn't detect the smell of alcohol, only the scent of her perfume. Nothing overpowering, just a light fragrance that reminded him of his mother's favorite lavender soap. That was definitely a switch from the women he'd known who bathed in expensive concoctions designed to turn on a man, when it only served to turn him off.

Logan climbed into the driver's seat, flipped on the overhead light and pulled his cell phone from the holder attached to the dash. "Do you want to call your father and let him know what's going on, or should I?"

"Good luck," she said. "He's in Chicago on business until tomorrow. And I gave the staff the night off."

"Anyone else I can call?"

"No."

Figured. That meant she was his sole responsibility for the time being. He shoved the phone back in the holder and released a rough sigh. "Then I guess it's you and me and the E.R."

She frowned. "Just drive me home and I'll be fine."

Not until he had a better look at the cut. When he reached over to remove the cloth, she physically jumped, as if he'd scared her out of her skin with a simple touch. "Relax," he told her as he lifted the makeshift bandage away. "I'm only trying to see how bad this is."

"It's a minor scrape," she said. "I got up close and personal with a wall outside the ladies' room when I tripped."

Obviously she hadn't bothered to check it out in a mirror. "It looks like it might need stitches. The hospital's not that far."

"No hospital." Her voice held an edge of panic. "I don't care for emergency rooms, or doctors."

She could be concerned the medical staff would run a tox screen, and that could pose a problem if the press got wind of an off-the-chart blood-alcohol level. Still, her condition might warrant treatment beyond mending a superficial cut, and right now she was Logan's responsibility. He lifted her hand from her lap and pressed it against the cloth again. "You could have a concussion."

"I'm certain I don't."

"Are you a doctor, Ms. Fordyce?"

"Are you, Mr. O'Brien?"

For the first time in his life, Logan wished he were. Then he could examine her, medically speaking, and take her home. Her home, not his. But medicine hadn't been his calling…and that gave him an idea. "Look, my brother *is* a doctor, and he only lives about ten minutes from here. He could probably check it out."

She mulled that over before saying, "I'll agree to this, but only if you promise to take me home afterward."

Not a problem, since that was his plan. "I'll give him a call and see if he's available."

Logan already knew he was. He'd spoken with Devin earlier in the evening and learned he had a rare day off from his duties as chief resident of trauma, which meant this request could cost him. Big-time.

He retrieved the cell phone again, hit the speed

dial and hoped he didn't wake the whole household, including the baby. Or worse, disturb his brother catching up on lost time between the sheets with his wife.

After two rings, Devin answered with his usual, "Dr. O'Brien."

"Hey, Dev, it's Logan. Sorry to call you so late."

"I'm still up, thanks to a kid who's decided it's playtime, not bedtime. What's going on?"

"I have a client who needs medical attention, but she's not too keen on going to the E.R." He sent Jenna a quick glance to find her staring out the windshield. "She has a cut on her forehead. Mind if I bring her by so you can take a look at it?"

Devin released a low laugh. "A client, huh? Are you charging for stud service these days?"

He was in no mood for his brother's attempt at humor. "I provide *driving* services for her. If you'll do this, I'll let you have my season tickets for the home game of your choice."

"Deal. But if it's something I can't handle in a nonhospital setting, then you're going to have to take her to the E.R."

That could pose a monumental challenge for Logan. But what choice did he have? "Agreed."

"Hang on a minute."

Logan could hear the sounds of muffled voices and realized Devin was consulting his wife. A few moments later, his brother came back to the phone and said, "Stacy's okay with it, on one condition, aside from the tickets. We do this at your condo, and I have to bring Sean with me. Car rides make him sleepy."

"Not a problem. I'll see you in a few minutes." And it wasn't a problem for Logan. He enjoyed being around his fifteen-month-old nephew, as long as he could send him home again. What he knew about taking care of a kid for more than a few hours could best be described with two words—not much. As far as taking Jenna to his place, that meant less of a drive. The faster he got this over with, the quicker he could get her back to the Fordyce mansion.

Logan snapped the phone closed and turned his attention back to Jenna. "He'll meet us at my apartment."

She kept her gaze trained on the dashboard. "Where do you live?"

"Downtown. A couple of miles from here."

"I appreciate this," she said. "I hope I'm not causing too much trouble."

"No trouble at all." And that wasn't exactly true. She could mean big trouble for Logan if he didn't stop noticing things about her, including the fact she had a great body, even if she was short. He needed to remember she was the daughter of a client. An important client who wouldn't appreciate any man having questionable thoughts about his daughter. Especially a man whom he trusted to do the right thing—and the right thing would be for Logan to keep his eyes, and his hands, to himself.

"Do you think I can take this cloth away now?" Jenna asked after he started the ignition. "My arm's getting tired."

"Let me see."

When she lowered the rag, Logan lifted her chin and brought her face toward him.

Okay, so she had soft skin and a really nice mouth. So did a lot of women. She probably had a hefty trust fund and an overblown sense of self-worth, too. Logan refused to head down that sorry road again.

"It's stopped bleeding, so you can take it off," he said as he returned his hands to the steering wheel and his mind back on business, where they belonged.

He drove back to the loft at a sluggish pace behind the weekend traffic and ill-timed lights. During the trip, Jenna kept her sunglasses in place and her gaze centered straight ahead until they pulled into the parking garage. Aside from a muttered, "thanks," when he helped her out of the Hummer and into the elevator, she remained silent. That was okay with Logan. He intended to keep their relationship on a strictly professional level. He also planned to keep his distance, but he didn't feel he could do that until they reached his apartment; the reason why he continued to hold on to her until he had her seated on the club chair in the living room.

"This seems like a nice place," she said, finally breaking the silence.

Searching for much-needed space, Logan dropped down on the sofa across from the chair. "I bought it from my sister and brother-in-law after they moved into their new house."

"Then you have one brother and one sister?"

"Actually, four brothers and a sister."

She smiled. "Wow. I'm an only child, so I can't imagine having such a large family. What are your parents like?"

Small talk was good. He could handle small talk. "They live in west Houston in the same middle-class neighborhood where I grew up." Heavy emphasis on "middle class." Logan wanted Jenna Fordyce to know up front that he hadn't originated from her side of the society divide, even if his financial situation had changed with his success.

When she made no move to take off her sunglasses, he said, "Feel free to get rid of the shades. I've been there before, so I'm not going to judge you."

She wrung her hands together several times. "The light bothers my eyes."

Man, he wouldn't want to be her in the morning. "If you think it's bad now, wait until tomorrow."

"Why's that?"

Obviously she'd never visited hangover central before, whereas, at one time, he'd been a frequent guest. "I take it you don't drink too often."

"No, I don't. I've never cared that much for alcohol. I only have a glass of wine on occasion."

That could explain her current state if she'd had more than a few tonight, but something still didn't quite ring true for Logan. Her speech didn't sound the least bit slurred. In fact, she sounded coherent. Probably one of the lucky ones who could drink and drown and still be able to fake sobriety.

When she grew silent again, Logan considered turning on the TV to watch the baseball game he'd recorded, but decided Ms. Fordyce didn't look like a baseball fan. He suspected tennis was her game, if sports interested her at all. For that reason, he should probably ask what she preferred, and right when he was about to pose the question, the doorbell rang, indicating help had arrived.

Logan pushed off the sofa, strode to the entry and opened the door to his brother who had a duffel bag hanging on one shoulder and a wide-eyed toddler wearing red superhero pajamas braced on one hip.

He stepped aside to let them in. "You made good time."

"The advantage of learning the fastest route when you're on call," Devin said. "Where's the patient?"

"Right down the hall."

When they reached the living room, Logan gestured toward his guest who had yet to acknowledge them. "Devin, this is Jenna Fordyce."

When Devin moved in front of the chair, Jenna offered her hand and a smile, something she hadn't done with Logan back at the bar. "It's a pleasure to meet you, Devin. I hope I'm not wasting your time."

"Not a problem," Devin said as he handed off Sean to Logan before taking Jenna's hand for a brief shake. He pulled up an ottoman in front of the chair and set his bag in his lap. "Now, let's take a look at that cut."

Logan hooked a thumb over his shoulder. "While you're doing that, I'll take the kid into the kitchen and see if I can find him a cookie."

Devin sent him a hard look. "Don't give him more than one. If I bring him home on a sugar high, you and I both are going to have to answer to my wife."

Logan had always considered his sister-in-law to be a reasonable woman, but he didn't want to test her. "I'll keep that in mind."

After he entered the adjacent kitchen, Logan held Sean high above his head, eliciting a laugh from his nephew. "You're getting heavy, bud," he said as he brought him back down and set him on the counter. "I only have a chocolate-chip cookie, so I hope that's okay."

Sean answered with the single word, *cookie*, and a wide grin, indicating Logan was definitely speaking his language.

When he opened the cabinet, withdrew the

cookie from the package and handed it to Sean, the kid squealed. One thing about it, toddlers could be easy to please, unlike several of the women Logan had known. One in particular. He wasn't sure why he kept thinking about his former fiancée tonight. The answer to that was sitting in the next room, undergoing an exam by his brother. But aside from Helena's and Jenna's similar backgrounds, he recognized several differences between the two, at least when it came to the physical aspects. Then again, he didn't plan to explore those differences. Once Devin was done doing his doctor thing, Logan would have Ms. Fordyce back at the family mansion in record time.

Sean finished the last bite of cookie and held out his hand, palm up, and wiggled his fingers. "More."

"Not a good idea, bud." Logan looked around for another form of entertainment and selected a wooden spoon sticking out from the jar holding utensils he rarely used. "How about practicing your batting swing with this? Just don't hit me."

Sean decided the spoon worked better as a drumstick and began pounding the cabinet without the least semblance of rhythm, spewing words that made little sense. But as long as it kept him happy, then that made Logan happy.

Remaining close to his nephew to prevent him from taking a spill, Logan leaned back against the counter and glanced at the pass-through opening that offered a view of the living room. Devin had taped up the cut with thin white strips and right then he was shining a penlight in her eyes. Logan could tell they were discussing something, but he couldn't make out a word with Sean now pounding the metal canisters.

A few minutes later, his nephew grew tired of playing musician and insisted on being held. Logan scooped him up into his arms where Sean rested his cheek on his shoulder. At least Devin could go home and tell Stacy that Uncle Logan had succeeded in wearing the kid out by giving him a spoon.

A few minutes later, Devin walked into the kitchen, sporting a somber expression. "I don't think she has a serious head injury, but someone needs to watch her tonight, in case she does have a slight concussion."

And that proved to be a major problem. "No one's at her house," Logan said. "If you're that worried, maybe she should be admitted to the hospital."

"And maybe you should let her stay in your guest room."

That wasn't in accordance with Logan's plan. "Not a good idea."

Devin frowned. "I've never known you to refuse a good-looking woman in distress."

"A drunk, good-looking woman who happens to be the kid of a billionaire client, and he sure as hell wouldn't appreciate me spending the night with his daughter."

Devin scrubbed a hand over the back of his neck and studied the floor. "She's not drunk, Logan. She's going blind."

Chapter Two

For the past year, Jenna Fordyce had lived in a world of shadows and solitude, and at times excruciating pain, both physically and emotionally. Yet the one night she'd chosen to venture outside her safe haven to celebrate her best friend's thirtieth birthday, she'd landed in a precarious situation—with a cut on her forehead and a possible concussion, being tended by an off-duty doctor in a strange man's apartment.

An exclusive apartment, Jenna had decided the minute she'd walked into the elevator on Logan O'Brien's arm. A very large apartment, she'd realized when they'd crossed the uncarpeted floor and she'd noticed the echo of their footsteps. She'd become skilled at discerning details by relying on other senses aside from sight, particularly sound. Right now she heard the murmur of low voices, and suspected she was most likely the topic of conversation. No doubt the doctor was informing his brother that she was practically blind, not under the influence.

The rapid shuffle of bare feet drew Jenna's complete attention. A child's feet, she decided, and confirmed that when she squinted against the light and saw a small figure standing before her, only a vague image viewed through the hazy film of her failing eyes. She felt the tiny hand resting on her wrist, and experienced the inherent maternal instinct that sent her arms open wide to welcome little Sean.

When he climbed into her lap and rested his cheek against her breast, Jenna laid her cheek on top of his head, inhaled his sweet after-bath scent, absorbed his warmth and turned her thoughts to another baby boy. The one who had recently been little more to her than a voice on the phone, a precious "I love you, Mommy," to carry her through the lonely days and nights. The gift that kept her going. And hoping.

"Nothing like making yourself right at home in the lady's lap, Sean."

Devin O'Brien's voice, Jenna determined. She'd

immediately found an affinity with the caring doctor. The jury was still out on the doctor's hardcase brother. "He's not bothering me, at all, Devin."

"That's because he's finally tired."

When Devin lifted Sean from her lap, Jenna wanted to ask him to wait a few more minutes. To give her a little more time to fill her empty arms and heart. She slid her glasses back into place, this time to hide the threatening tears. "May I go home now?"

"You're going to stay here with me tonight."

Logan's commanding voice made Jenna bristle. "That's not necessary."

"Doctor's orders," Devin added in a more even tone. "Logan told me you'd be spending the night alone, and we'd both feel better if you had some company, in case you have any problems from the injury."

Maybe Devin would feel better, but Jenna doubted Logan shared that opinion. He probably wished she'd never had the bouncer call for a driver. Frankly, she wished she'd called a cab, which she could still do now.

She took a moment to weigh her options, all two of them. She could insist on going home and hope for the best, or stay and know someone would be there if she did suffer latent effects from the fall. She'd fought hard to maintain as much independence as possible, but under the current circumstances, she had no choice but to give up some of that hard-won freedom. The price she had to pay for taking a foolish risk. "Okay, I'll stay."

"Good," Devin said. "And you don't have to worry about Logan. He has a guest room upstairs, and he's a decent guy. Although, I'm much better looking."

"And married, Dev. Now, go home to your wife."

Logan's tone held a touch of amusement, something he evidently reserved for family members only, Jenna decided. He certainly hadn't sounded the least bit amused since the moment he'd become her reluctant escort. "Thanks for everything, Devin."

"You're welcome. Tell Jenna good-night, Sean."

"Night, night," came the childlike voice, followed by a soft baby kiss on her cheek, filling Jenna with more yearning and more memories. "Good night, sweetie. Sleep tight."

She listened with longing to Sean's toddler babble and the brotherly banter as the trio left the room. But when she heard the final goodbyes and the closing door in the distance, she was overcome with a solid case of jitters.

Logan O'Brien made her nervous, and it wasn't due to his imposing height; she was much shorter than most men. It wasn't even the edge in his voice, or his stoic demeanor. His overt, man-in-control attitude made her wary. Many a woman might be drawn to that take-charge aura, but she didn't intend to count herself among them.

"We need to talk."

The deep timbre of Logan's voice startled Jenna, causing her hand to flutter to her throat. "I didn't realize you were back."

She heard the scrape of furniture immediately before Logan came somewhat into view. "I'm right here. Now, explain to me why you didn't tell me you can't see."

Logan O'Brien pulled no punches, and normally Jenna would find that refreshing. But not necessarily in this instance. "I don't usually greet strangers with 'Hi, my name's Jenna Fordyce. I'm as blind as that proverbial bat.'"

"That only accounts for our initial meeting, not for the rest of the time we've been together," he said. "Try again."

She wasn't certain how to explain, aside from handing him the truth. "Tonight was the first time I've been out of the house for months, socially speaking. I wanted to be viewed as normal, and spared the usual pity." At least for a while.

"How long have you been this way?"

"A total recluse or a sassy pants, as my mother used to say?" Before her mother had been taken from her, when Jenna had just turned thirteen.

He released an impatient sigh. "How long have you had problems with your vision?"

Longer than she cared to recall. "I was diagnosed with a form of corneal dystrophy when I was in my early teens. At first, it wasn't too bad, aside from the eye infections, but I've always known it would continue to progress."

"Exactly how much can you see?"

"Not much. It's a little like looking through shattered, cloudy glass. Everything's distorted. I can see shapes, but no real details. Or I can when I'm not wearing sunglasses."

He reached up and pulled the shades away, something Jenna preferred he hadn't done. Since Devin had dimmed the lights earlier, she wasn't too concerned over her photosensitivity. She was worried about how her eyes would appear to him.

"Can you see me better now?" he asked.

"I can tell you're sitting in front of me, but that's about it."

"And there's not one damn procedure in this day and time that will help you?"

He sounded as frustrated as Jenna often felt, and she found that remarkable, coming from a man she'd just met. "A corneal transplant is the only cure."

"And that involves finding a donor," he said.

"Yes. I've been waiting over a year. Of course, if it were up to my father, he'd try to buy a set of corneas. Or at the very least, wield his influence to have me moved up on the list."

"But you won't let him."

She shook her head. "That wouldn't be fair. I've spent a good deal of my life as a sighted person when there are people waiting who've never had that advantage. Some are even children. They should be first in line."

"That's an admirable attitude."

She shifted slightly. "Before you start thinking I'm ready for sainthood, you have to understand that having a transplant isn't something I take lightly. Sometimes it scares me to think about it. But I'm willing to wait." Wait for someone to die in order to see, a fact Jenna tried not to dwell on. If she had only herself to consider, she would accept her limitations and forget the procedure. She'd use her cane all the time and consider finding a guide dog. But she had a three-and-a-half-year-old son counting on her, even if several hundred miles had separated them for the past few months.

"If you have the transplant, your vision will be restored completely?" Logan asked.

"That's what I'm hoping." Although, she would also be facing possible tissue rejection and the chance that the disease could return in a few years' time following the transplant.

"That's got to be tough. I can't imagine not being able to see."

"I've learned to compensate by thinking about what I'll do when I can see again." Being able to care for her child was top priority. "In the meantime, I have to rely on developing mental portraits using other senses. I'll demonstrate, if you'll let me touch you."

"Oh, yeah?" She could hear the smile in his voice.

Jenna released a shaky laugh when she realized how suggestive that sounded. "I meant, I want to touch your face to get a better idea of what you look like, if that's okay."

"What if you're disappointed?"

She shrugged. "Honestly, I've learned that true character has nothing to do with physical attractiveness. I just like to have a frame of reference."

"Then, go ahead," he said. "Touch away."

Jenna was a little unnerved by the provocative quality of his voice, but not enough to discourage her. "My depth perception is nonexistent, so you're going to have to help me. I'll start with your hair and work my way down."

When she held out her hands and closed her eyes, he placed her hands on either side of his temples. She feathered her fingertips through his hair—a nice, thick head of hair. "You're definitely not going bald."

"Not that I've noticed."

"What color is your hair?" she asked.

"Black."

He had the "tall" and "dark" down, and the time had come to verify the "handsome." Jenna began by outlining his forehead with her fingertips before brushing her thumbs over his brows. "What about your eyes?"

"They're blue."

Her artistic nature took over. "Sky-blue? Aqua-blue? Cobalt?"

"I've never thought about it before. I guess, sky-blue." He sounded somewhat self-conscious, and Jenna found that endearing coming from such a macho guy.

"Most people take the details for granted," she said, though she never had. "That's quite a striking contrast, black hair and light-blue eyes."

"My mother's half Armenian, and my father's Irish. I'm a mix of both."

"Interesting." And so was his nose that she now examined. When she contacted a slight indentation on the right side of the bridge, she asked, "What happened here?"

"I jumped out of an airplane and landed on my face."

"Seriously?" she asked around her shock.

He released a low, sexy laugh. "I got hit by a pitch when I was up to bat during a high-school baseball game. I thought the skydiving thing sounded more interesting."

She wasn't surprised he'd been a jock, but she was taken aback by his sudden show of humor. She wasn't surprised by the strength of his jaw, covered by whiskers that lightly abraded her palms, but the creases along his cheeks threw her a bit. "You have dimples."

"Unfortunately, yes."

She smiled. "Unfortunately? Women love dimples. It gives a man a boyish quality."

"If you say so," he said with extreme skepticism.

While she traced his full lips with a fingertip, Jenna put all the finer points together, creating a mental sculpture that probably wouldn't do justice to the real thing. But she'd discerned enough to know that he was definitely attractive.

And absolutely masculine, she realized when she ran her fingers over his prominent Adam's apple and down his corded neck that ended beneath stretchy knit. "You're wearing a T-shirt." She dropped her hands to his thighs. "And jeans." She found his foot with her own foot and gave it a nudge. "Boots, but not the cowboy kind. Hiking boots. You're an outdoorsman. Do you like to hike?"

"Yeah. Hiking and camping. But with the job, I haven't been in a few years."

Her mind wandered back to a better time, a better place, when she'd still had her sight. "I used to hike quite a bit when I was younger."

"How old are you now?"

Although his query was abrupt, and some might say inappropriate, Jenna liked his no-holds-barred attitude. It certainly beat having people view her as too fragile. "I turned thirty last month. And you?"

"Thirty-four."

She hid an unexpected yawn behind her hand. "Now that I've gotten to know you better, I suppose I can comfortably spend the night with you."

"Are you ready to go to bed now?"

She grinned. "I don't know you *that* well."

He cleared his throat. "I meant, are you ready for me to show you to the guest room."

"I'm teasing. I knew what you meant. You go to your bed, I go to mine."

"When you put it that way, it doesn't sound too damn appealing, does it?"

"No, it doesn't."

The sudden onset of silence was heavy, almost stifling. The undeniable tension passing between them required no visual confirmation, only instinct. And Jenna had always had good instincts, even before she'd lost her vision. But as much as she would like to throw caution aside, maybe offer Logan O'Brien a little encouragement, her intuition warned her to back off, before she made another mistake tonight.

When she realized she still had one hand planted on Logan's thigh, she drew it back as if she'd suffered an electrical jolt. In many ways, she had. "Does your guest room happen to have a TV?"

"Just a bed. I don't have many guests."

At least not any guests that required their own bed, Jenna surmised. "Do you have a TV in here?"

"A forty-two-inch plasma. Why?"

Of course he would ask that question. Why would a blind woman be interested in something she couldn't see? "I like to have a TV turned on when I go to bed. The sound helps me sleep."

"I know what you mean. I usually fall asleep watching sports right here in the living room."

"Then the living room it is. Just show me to the sofa and turn on the TV."

He took her hand and helped her to her feet. "I'll make a deal with you. Since I've been instructed by my brother to keep an eye on you, you can have the sofa and I'll sleep in the lounger."

"You really don't have to do that. I'm feeling fine. No nausea. No dizziness." Not exactly true. Knowing he was so close made her a little light-headed.

"Look, Jenna, unless you're going to trust me enough to sleep in the same bed with you, then you're going to have to deal with me staying in the living room so I can watch you."

She wasn't certain she could trust *herself* to sleep in the same bed with him. "Okay, but you don't have to watch me all night."

He ran a fingertip along her cheek. "I have no problem watching you all night."

Jenna experienced a rush of inexplicable heat and a round of regret that she couldn't see him. But she'd felt the softness of his touch, sensed his gaze and, for the first time in a long time, felt like a normal—and desirable—woman.

* * *

Jenna Fordyce was one hell of a stubborn woman, something Logan had discovered when she'd rejected his offer to assist her while she got ready for bed. Right now she was in the downstairs half bath putting on the T-shirt he'd loaned her, while he waited outside the door, hoping she didn't fall again. And that was probably just as well. Watching her dress was a bad idea.

Her earlier exploration had brought about a physical reaction that he couldn't ignore. He also couldn't discard her attitude about her condition, which had been nothing short of amazing. He was having a hard time ignoring her, period.

Still, he didn't particularly like that she'd failed to tell the truth about her vision problems and he couldn't help but wonder what else she might be hiding. He hated deception of any kind, even more so due to his ex-fiancée's betrayal. But after Jenna had explained her reasons for not telling him the truth, he'd understood her motivation on some level. He *didn't* understand why he was so damned attracted to her. Of course, she was a great-looking woman, but that wasn't all. He admired her need for independence and appreciated her insecurities. She might have been robbed of her sight, but she probably saw a lot more than most people who had twenty-twenty vision. She'd definitely seen more in him than most women, without evening knowing what he looked like.

And that pretty much answered his question. Throw all those traits into the mix, and you had a remarkable woman wrapped up in a petite package. Regardless, his post-Helena burn had yet to heal, and the last thing he wanted was another female complication. Jenna Fordyce didn't strike him as a one-night-stand kind of girl, and, lately, that's all that had interested him. No commitments. No promises. Nothing that even remotely resembled a steady relationship.

He also didn't need Jenna hurting herself again, exactly what Logan feared she'd done when a clattering sound filtered through the closed door. He rapped his knuckles on the facing and called, "Are you okay in there?" And if she didn't answer in two seconds, he was going to break down the door.

"I'm fine," she said. "I dropped the toothbrush in the sink and knocked over the toothpaste."

At least she hadn't dropped onto the floor. "Do you need anything?"

"Not unless you happen to have some eye-makeup remover."

He very well could. But he was tempted to deny it in order to avoid having to explain. Then again, if she really needed it, he should give it to her. "Are you decent?"

"That's debatable, but you can come in."

Logan opened the door to find her wearing the threadbare T-shirt that hit her midthigh, standing in front of the mirror and rubbing a washcloth over her face. Ignoring the clothes piled on the marble counter—including a skimpy lace bra—he strode to the vanity, opened the drawer, pulled out the metallic-gold makeup bag and rifled through it. And he'd be damned if he didn't find exactly what she was looking for.

He withdrew the blue bottle and put in her hand. "Here you go. Eye-makeup remover."

She frowned. "Is there something you're not telling me about yourself, Logan?"

"I don't wear makeup, if that's what you're asking. It belongs to someone else."

"You have a girlfriend."

"I have an *ex*-girlfriend."

"I see." She opened the lid and dabbed the washcloth with the clear liquid. "But you've kept a few reminders."

"Yeah. To remind me of one of the many reasons why we're not together anymore. She wore too much makeup."

"Okay."

Logan expected Jenna to question his other reasons, but she concentrated on removing the mascara. He liked that she hadn't grilled him. Liked that she'd let past history remain in the past. He liked her a lot and couldn't remember the last time he'd felt that way about a woman.

She blew out a frustrated sigh. "I should never

have let Candice put makeup on me. It's a pain in the butt, and if I don't get it off, it could cause problems." Then she turned to him and asked, "Is it gone, or am I ready for Halloween four months early?"

"Let me help." He took the cloth from her hand, clasped her chin and wiped at the smudges beneath her lower lids. He was very aware of their close proximity. Aware that she wasn't wearing a bra beneath the shirt, and that particular knowledge was creating major havoc on his body. If he didn't get away now, he was in danger of kissing her.

On that thought, he tossed the rag into the sink and backed up a step. "It's all gone. And you don't need any makeup."

She smiled. "I bet you say that to all the women you rescue from the clutches of evil mascara."

"This is a first. I've never intentionally taken off a woman's makeup."

"I'm sure you're very good at removing lipstick."

"Could be." And if she had any on now, which she didn't, he'd be glad to remove it for her. "Are you finished?"

She pushed her hair back with one hand. "I believe I am. Are you?"

When he realized how close he was coming to making a fatal error, Logan took her by the arm and guided her back into the living room to settle her on the sofa. "Stretch out and I'll cover you up."

After she complied, Logan pulled the blanket up to her chin, concealing her body and giving him some much-needed relief. "Is that okay?"

She worked her arms from underneath the covers. "It's fine. Are you okay?"

"Yeah. Why?"

"I don't know. You sound almost angry."

"I'm not angry." At least not at her.

She stretched her arms above her head before folding them beneath her breasts. "Then you're not going to boot me out on my butt after I fall asleep?"

"You're safe." But if she knew what he was thinking—that he'd like to climb on that couch with her—she might be the one doing the booting.

After grabbing up the remote from the coffee table, Logan switched on the TV. "Any particular show you want to watch?"

"It doesn't matter to me, as long as there's audio. You decide."

A return to his regularly scheduled program might offer a solid distraction. "I recorded the baseball game. They were in extra innings when I left to pick you up."

"I know. I also know the score. I heard some guys talking at the bar."

He set the remote back on the table. "Don't tell me or you'll ruin it."

"I'll let you be surprised, then." She rolled to her side to face him and began twisting the corner of the blanket. "Before you settle in for the night, there's something I need to ask you."

Jenna's tone was so somber, he worried that maybe she wasn't feeling well. Worried that he might have to make a trip to the E.R. after all. But her well-being mattered more than the inconvenience. "What's wrong?"

"Nothing's wrong." She closed her lids, then opened them slowly. "It's been a long time since I've seen myself in the mirror, and I want to know if my eyes—"

"They're as beautiful as the rest of you." And they were—pale brown, round eyes framed by long, dark lashes. No, she didn't need any makeup. She was perfect just the way she was. Maybe even too perfect.

Jenna smiled, but to Logan it looked almost sad. "I bet you say that to all the blind girls who end up on your sofa."

"You're the first, and it's the truth."

When she reached out her hand, he took it without hesitation. "Thanks, Logan. I'm glad we met."

"So am I." And he was, more than he cared to admit. "Now, get some sleep."

He gave her hand a squeeze and took his place in the lounger several feet away. He tried to concentrate on the game, but he was too busy analyzing the woman on his couch. He wondered if she was as real as she seemed. If everything she'd told him was accurate. If he'd misjudged her due to his own bitter experience. He suspected he had, and he wanted more proof.

For Logan O'Brien, the night might have begun with an unwelcome interruption, but it had ended with one huge surprise—Jenna Fordyce.

Chapter Three

"What are you doing?"

At the sound of Logan's distinct and somewhat gruff voice, Jenna turned and leaned back against the kitchen counter. "I was going to make you breakfast to repay you for rescuing me last night. But I've never been much of a cook, even before I lost my sight." She felt behind her for the carton of milk and held it up. "Can I interest you in cold cereal?"

"No thanks."

Jenna detected a hint of irritation in his tone. "Is something wrong?"

"When I didn't find you on the couch after I took my shower, I was worried."

She appreciated his concern, even if it wasn't warranted. "You don't have any reason to worry." She touched the edge of the bandage covering her wound. "My head's a little sore, but I'm fine."

Jenna calculated Logan's approach through the sound of his footsteps, and knew he moved beside her when she caught the trace scent of fresh soap. "As soon as you get dressed, we can leave," he said.

She ran a fast hand down the T-shirt he'd loaned her last night. "This is comfortable. Think I'll just wear it home. I'll have it laundered and back to you next week." Better still, she could deliver it in person.

Not a banner idea. She had no cause to pursue a relationship with a man at this point in her life.

"It looks good on you," he said. "But if you keep it, then you'll have to explain to your father where the shirt came from. And that would lead to telling him you spent the night with me and, in turn, I'll lose his business."

Always seeing things through a business lens, just like her father. "He's not due home until late afternoon, so don't concern yourself with getting caught. Which reminds me. What time is it now?"

"Almost ten."

"I can't believe I slept so late." But then, she hadn't slept all that well last night knowing Logan had been only a few paces away.

"And that's why we need to get a move on," he said. "Before Avery finds out you've been gone all night."

Jenna wouldn't be surprised if her dad had already called home only to connect to the voice mail. "My personal life isn't my father's business, and what happened last night doesn't qualify as questionable. I slept on your couch, and you kept watch over me from a chair."

"I still plan to have you home well before he arrives." He caught her hand and wrapped it firmly in his. "Come on. I'll help you get dressed."

Plainly, he was more than ready to be rid of her. "I can dress myself, thank you."

"I'll hang around, anyway, to make sure you're okay."

"Suit yourself."

Jenna allowed Logan to guide her into the bathroom where she took care of her morning ritual while he played watchdog outside the door. She managed to slide the blouse over her head, but when she attempted to close the skirt's back zipper, it wouldn't budge. At times like these, she wished she had a closet full of shapeless shifts and elastic waistbands, or the return of her sight.

Only one option existed at the moment—swallowing her pride. "I need some help, Logan."

The door creaked open. "What's wrong?"

"Nothing serious," she said, keeping her back to him. "Just a malfunctioning zipper. And if you're like most guys, you've had a lot of practice with women's zippers."

"I'm better at lowering them, but I'll give it a shot."

Though his voice held a touch of amusement, Jenna couldn't quite shake the sudden images his comment evoked as he moved behind her. "If you can't fix it, then I guess I'll have to wear your shirt home, after all."

"I can handle it." Bracing his hand on her hips, he tugged her toward him and went to work.

After only a single attempt, Jenna felt the zipper dislodge, followed by Logan saying, "You're all set."

She turned to thank him, swayed forward and in order to right herself, landed her hands on a wide expanse of powerhouse bare chest. "You're not wearing a shirt." A brilliant observation on her part.

He clasped her waist. "You have my shirt."

Clearly, her brain's command center didn't feel the need to remove her hands. "If that's the only shirt you own, you need to ask my father for more money."

"I own several shirts. I just haven't put one on, yet."

She'd found that out the pleasant way. "I see. Or maybe it's because I don't see. You could be naked, and I'd never know."

"I'm not naked." He shifted closer. "I'm wearing a smile."

Without thought, her hands drifted down his firm sides until she contacted a denim waistband. "Very funny. You really had me fooled for a minute."

"Anything else you need from me?"

She could think of several things, most of which wouldn't be wise. Interesting, yes. Prudent, no. Reluctantly, she dropped her arms to her sides. "I should probably go home now. I need to take a shower."

"I have a shower, and I'd be glad to help."

How simple it would be to take him up on the offer. How very easy to forget why she couldn't acknowledge this overriding chemistry between them. "Believe me, I've showered by myself before. Every morning, in fact."

"Fine, but if you decide on the way home that you'd like my assistance, just let me know."

"Do you know where you're going, Logan?"

Straight into a ditch if he didn't keep his eyes on the road and off of her. "I've been to your place before."

"Really? When was that?"

He glanced at Jenna to find her frowning. "About two years ago, when I first contracted with your dad. He invited me to a dinner party."

"Apparently, I wasn't in attendance at that little soiree."

"No, you weren't there." Without a doubt, he would've remembered if she had been.

"I must have been busy, otherwise I'm sure I would have been playing the perfect hostess to my father's perfect corporate crusader." Her sarcasm was unmistakable.

"You don't sound like you enjoy that scene," he said.

"Not really, but I view it as a favor to my father."

Logan could relate to family loyalty. "What else do you do in your spare time these days, aside from being a hostess?"

"I listen to audio books, mostly nonfiction, although I do enjoy a good legal thriller now and then. I've been learning Braille and several foreign languages, and when Calvin's not carting me to doctor's appointments, he drives me to the library twice a week where I tell stories to preschoolers."

He wasn't all that surprised by the revelation, although he was impressed. "I could tell you like being around kids when I saw you with my nephew."

"Yes, I do." She sighed. "They don't pass judgment or patronize me. Basically they view me as a storyteller who happens to be blind, not the other way around."

He sensed that was important to her—being treated like an average person. As far as Logan was concerned, Jenna Fordyce was anything but average.

"What do you do when you're not working?" she asked.

"I go to sporting events when I have some spare time. And on Sunday, I have lunch with the family."

Although, he'd missed those gatherings several times over the past few months, something that didn't sit well with his mother.

"That means you're going to be late to your lunch because of me," she said.

"It's not going to matter if I'm late." He would receive more grief from his sister for not jumping back into the dating loop, and from his brothers who claimed he'd lost his touch with women. Come to think of it, he could remedy that harassment—at least, temporarily—with one suggestion. "Since Avery won't be back until later, you should come with me. The food's simple, but the company's good."

When she didn't immediately respond, Logan glanced in her direction to find her deep in thought. "Well?" he asked.

"I should stay home in case he arrives early." She sent him an apologetic smile. "Thanks for the offer, but I'll have to pass."

Logan couldn't explain his disappointment, nor did he want to acknowledge it. But he did feel it. "Not a problem."

The conversation waned for the next few miles until Logan approached the estate—a house that looked as if it could hold five families. "We're at the entrance," he said as they pulled into the drive.

Jenna rummaged through her purse and withdrew a remote control, pointed it straight ahead and sent the security gate in motion.

Logan drove through the entry and immediately noticed a man with silver hair dressed in a black business suit, standing on the front porch. The last man he wanted to see at the moment.

Slowing the vehicle to a crawl, he asked, "How well do you and your dad get along?"

She rubbed her forehead, like the question had given her a major headache. "As long as he doesn't try to tell me what to do, we get along fine. He's very overprotective, the consummate doting father. But I love him with all my heart and appreciate all he's done for me since my mother's death. I probably don't tell him that enough."

"Well, now's your chance."

She turned her head toward him, a confused look on her face. "I don't understand."

Maybe not, but she would. And whether Avery Fordyce would understand why his only daughter had been out all night, still remained to be seen. "Looks like your father caught an earlier flight." And right then Avery looked as if he could fly off the porch and put someone in a choke hold.

Jenna tipped her head back against the seat and muttered, "Great," while Logan navigated the circular drive. After stopping underneath the portico, he said, "Let me handle this."

"No. I'll handle it."

Logan had barely left the Hummer and reached the passenger side before Jenna had the door open, one leg dangling out of the vehicle.

After he guided her up the steps, he started to launch into an explanation but lost the opportunity when Avery asked, "Where in God's name have you been, Jenna?"

"She's been with me," Logan said, although Avery didn't look too pleased by the disclosure.

Jenna reached out to find her father's arm, leaned forward and kissed his cheek. "I went out for Candice's birthday and I had a little mishap." She touched the bandage on her forehead. "Logan was kind enough to have his brother, Devin, who happens to be a doctor, take a look at the cut. He fixed me up with a few little strips to hold it together, Logan loaned me his sofa for the night, end of story."

Avery scowled. "That's not the end of the story. Candice called Sasha this morning, and Sasha, in turn, called me. They were both worried sick because you didn't come home and you didn't bother to call."

Jenna lifted her chin in defiance. "I'll explain everything to Candice later, and I told Sasha to take the weekend off."

"My employees are loyal, Jenna." Avery directed a hard look at Logan. "They do as I ask, and I asked her to watch out for you."

"I'm thirty years old, Dad. I don't need a keeper."

"Apparently, you do, daughter."

Logan opted to intervene before all out warfare began between parent and child. "Jenna spending the night at my place was all my idea, Avery. She wanted to come home, but I wouldn't let her."

"And this is supposed to satisfy me?" He topped off the comment with an acid glare.

At this rate, he'd find himself minus an important client. "Devin and I decided she shouldn't be alone, in case she showed signs of a concussion."

"Which I didn't," Jenna added. "Now, let's go inside and let Logan get on with his business."

"Yes, let's go inside," Avery said. "You still have a lot of explaining to do."

Logan witnessed a spark of anger in Jenna's expression. "We can talk later, Dad. I have to have a shower so I can be ready when Logan takes me to his parents' for lunch. What time should I expect you, Logan?"

He couldn't determine who was more shocked—him or Fordyce. "Are you sure you want to go?"

She sent him a bright smile. "Of course. The very accommodating Sasha can look after Dad this afternoon while I'm with you."

Logan recognized pure and simple rebellion, and that he was stuck in the middle of a family battle. He could rescind the offer and insult Jenna, putting himself back in Avery's good graces. Or he could possibly piss off one of his biggest financial benefactors and spend the afternoon with that benfactor's daughter.

He glanced at the sullen Avery before turning his attention to Jenna, who had one of the greatest smiles he'd ever seen on a woman. Business versus pleasure. He chose pleasure. "I'll be back in about an hour."

Without waiting for Avery's response, Logan sprinted to the Hummer and drove off, wondering all the way home what in the hell he was doing.

"Do you know what you're doing, Jenna?"

Although she couldn't see her father's expression, she'd heard the disapproval in his tone. "I'm going to get ready to have lunch with Logan."

As she continued down the hall toward her bedroom, her father moved in front of her, halting her progress. "What do you really know about him?"

The classic fatherly lecture. Despite her limited eyesight, she should have seen it coming. "I know that you trust him. I also know he was very kind to me last night and a perfect gentleman, if that's your concern."

"He's a ladies' man. He's not the kind to settle for only one woman, especially a…"

His words trailed off, but his message came through loud and clear. "A woman like me, Dad? Isn't that what you meant to say?"

"You're special, Jenna."

"I'm going blind, Dad. My eyesight might be

bad, but that doesn't mean I can't enjoy a man's company. Even a 'ladies' man.' And this is only a casual lunch between friends. Logan didn't want me to be alone since I assumed Sasha wouldn't be here, and you wouldn't be home until much later."

"I don't want you to get hurt, sweetheart."

His gentle tone helped ease her resentment. "I'll only get hurt if I let him hurt me, and I won't. Besides, I'm not looking for anything permanent. You should know that by now."

"Yes, I know. Your divorce from David proved that. I wish the two of you would have tried a little harder."

"Don't, Dad. We're not having that discussion again." They'd worn out that territory three years ago.

"I can't talk you out of going to this lunch? We could have a nice afternoon together."

She reached out to pat his cheek. "We can have a nice evening together. You can tell me all about Chicago, and I can tell you how to inquire about the bathroom in Italian and French."

"You're still determined to take that European trip."

"Only after I have the transplants." If she ever had the transplants. "I'd also like to wait until John David's a little older so he can appreciate the culture."

"Have you told Logan about him?"

"The opportunity hasn't arisen yet." She planned to take the opportunity before day's end. "As

I've said, this is only a one-time event, not a prospective-daddy interview. J.D. already has a father."

"Again, I don't want you to—"

"Get hurt. I know, Dad." She drew him into a long embrace. "And I appreciate your concern. But you don't have to worry. I'm a big girl now."

"I know, Jenna, but I still worry about you. I've worried about you since the day you came into our lives."

"And if I'd been able to handpick my parents, I couldn't have chosen any better than you and Mother." Even if she'd often wondered that if they'd known her vision would eventually fail, would they have adopted her?

"And we couldn't have been more blessed to have you," he said, dispelling her doubts, and that earned him another hug.

"I love you, Dad," she said. "And please stop worrying. I can manage Logan O'Brien."

At one time, Logan had been able to manage Avery Fordyce by praising his business acumen, yielding to his demands and leading him to believe he had complete control. But that was before he'd met the man's daughter.

Under normal circumstances, Logan would have expected to be greeted by a member of the household staff. Nothing about this situation remotely resembled normal, the reason why he wasn't surprised when Avery answered the door with a curt, "Come in."

Logan followed Avery inside the house, hoping to discover Jenna waiting nearby so they could get the hell out of there. But the expansive foyer was deserted, with the exception of a few pieces of pricey artwork and Fordyce, who turned and said, "I don't like this, O'Brien."

Logan didn't have to ask what Avery didn't like. "It's only lunch."

"So you say. Just remember, Jenna means everything to me, son. She's an exceptional young woman. Fragile in many ways. If you mess with her feelings, you mess with mine. Understood?"

Avery's meaning couldn't be clearer if he'd carved it into stone—or into Logan's flesh. Still, Logan had a hard time believing Jenna was as fragile as her father had claimed. But if he screwed up with Avery's only child, he'd be out in the cold when it came to future contracts. "Understood."

"Now that you know what I expect, you may wait for Jenna in the study." He pointed to his right before pivoting around like a drill sergeant and heading down the lengthy hall.

Logan wandered into the room Avery had indicated, expecting to find a collection of books stacked on rows of shelves, maybe even an office setup. Instead, the area held a grouping of casual rattan furniture and plenty of pictures, but not the kind displayed in a trendy gallery. Portraits depicting a dark-haired boy spanned the length of the room. One showed a sleeping newborn lying on a blue blanket; another featured a toothless, smiling infant on his belly in a field of wildflowers, and beside that, a toddler dressed in a red baseball uniform with a miniature wooden bat.

Even if he didn't know the kid's identity, Logan suspected he was someone special. Possibly a member of the extended family—or immediate family.

"His name is John David."

He turned at the sound of the familiar voice to discover Jenna standing in the open doorway wearing a pale yellow, sleeveless dress, her dark hair secured atop her head. The sunshades covering her eyes and the white cane in her hand were the only indications she was anything but a healthy, beautiful woman. In fact, she looked so damn good, for a moment Logan had trouble responding to her comment. "Who took all these pictures?"

"I did. I used to own a small photography studio in northwest Houston before my eyes started giving me grief. I consider these portraits some of my best work."

That explained the quality of the photos, even if it didn't explain Jenna's relationship to the child, although Logan had his suspicions. "You must have really liked this particular subject."

"More than you know." She crossed the room, removed a framed photo from a table before returning and offering it for his inspection. "This one's my favorite."

Logan studied the picture of Jenna turned profile to the boy, their foreheads touching. The perfect depiction of a woman's fondness for a child. Or maybe a mother's love for her son. Then again, he could be mistaken since she hadn't mentioned having a child, nor had her father in the years he'd known him. But when he turned his attention from the photo to Jenna and saw the moisture dampening her cheeks, Logan sensed he was on the right track. And affirmation came when she said, "He's my son."

She raised the glasses and swept a fast hand beneath her eyes before replacing the shades again. "I'm sorry. It's very difficult to talk about him without my emotions going haywire."

Although he was tempted to ask exactly what had happened to the boy, Logan decided not to pressure Jenna for more information than she was willing or able to give. Instead, he said the only thing he could think to say. "He looks like you."

She gave him a tentative smile. "He definitely inherited my brown eyes, but his hair is lighter, like his dad's. Or it was the last time I could see it."

"How long ago was that?"

"He's three and a half now, so that would have been about a year ago, right before my vision took a severe turn for the worse. He went to live with his father not long after that. We share joint custody."

At least Jenna hadn't suffered a traumatic loss of her child, although Logan couldn't imagine how she'd tolerated a year without him. "When will he be back with you?"

She clutched the frame to her breasts, as if she were holding her absent son. "As soon as I have the corneal transplants. Since he's so active, I thought it best he stay with his dad a little longer than the usual six months. But it's been difficult since he's so far away."

"How far?"

"In Tennessee, outside of Memphis. I do talk to him every night, though."

A sorry substitute for physical contact. "I'm surprised Avery never mentioned him to me." Most grandfathers Logan had known doted over the grandchildren, including his own father.

"It's not that Dad doesn't love J.D.," she said. "In fact, he adores him. But he's never accepted the fact that J.D.'s father and I divorced."

Logan could see how that wouldn't go over well with a traditionalist like Avery Fordyce. Or his own parents, who'd had a hard time with his sister's divorce. "How long were you together?"

"I'd known him four years, and we'd been living together for three when I found out I was pregnant. We married five weeks later. Right after J.D. turned six months old, we realized it wasn't going to work. But David's a good father, and that's all that matters."

From the sadness in Jenna's tone, Logan gathered that maybe the divorce hadn't been her idea. He wanted to ask if she'd loved this David and if the guy had treated her well. If he'd accepted her blindness, or if that had been the reason for the split. "I guess marrying for the sake of a child isn't always a good thing." And he'd almost found himself caught in that trap.

She shook her head. "No, it's not. Particularly if two people are less than compatible, something we should have realized in three years. But sometimes you get stuck in a comfort zone with no desire to leave. Unfortunately, accidents happen, although I wouldn't change anything as far as my son's concerned."

Uncomfortable with the course of the conversation, Logan decided to turn the topic to their plans for the day. "Are you ready to go now?"

"Do you still want me to go?"

"Yeah. Any reason why I wouldn't?"

"I could think of several reasons why you might reconsider. Introducing a blind, divorcée with a child to your parents, for one."

"My parents aren't judgmental, Jenna." In fact, they would probably fall in love with her after five minutes in her company—and immediately start jumping to conclusions.

She shifted slightly. "There's also that little issue of my father, who is now in the den, sulking. He's worried you're going to seduce me, and I won't see it coming. Literally."

"I promise I'll behave myself." A promise he hoped he could keep.

Chapter Four

"Do your parents know you're bringing a guest?" When Jenna received no response except the click of a blinker, she reached across the seat and touched Logan's arm. "Are you all right?"

"Yeah. I'm fine."

She had some reservations about that, particularly since he'd been quiet since they'd begun the drive. "Did you hear my question?"

"You said something about my parents."

Evidently his mind was elsewhere. "I asked if they know I'm coming."

"I called my mother and told her I was bringing a friend. She was so glad to hear it, I don't think she'd care if I brought an army of hairy bikers."

Or a blind woman. "When was the last time you brought someone home?"

"It's been a while. I haven't made the Sunday lunches for a few months. Work's been kicking my butt."

Jenna predicted there was much more to his absences aside from work. "Then, you didn't tell her any details about me?"

"What do you mean?"

She wasn't sure if he was being evasive because he had told his mother, or he hadn't. "Did you mention I have a penchant for bumping into walls?"

"Sure. I told them you were a klutz and to secure anything breakable."

His teasing tone brought about Jenna's smile. "Seriously."

"My parents are smart people. They'll figure it out, and it won't matter to them."

Jenna hoped they didn't treat her any differently than they would any guest, and realized she would soon find out when Logan proclaimed, "We're here."

While Logan helped her from the SUV, Jenna gave herself a good mental scolding for her sudden case of nerves. She had no reason to be anxious. After all, following lunch, she would probably never encounter these people again.

With his hand firmly planted at her elbow, he

guided her into the backyard where the scents of charcoal and the hum of jubilant conversation calmed her nerves and buoyed her spirits. Then came the chorus of cheers and applause as the group converged on them. To Jenna, they appeared as a sea of ill-defined figures, but she didn't dare take off her glasses due to the summer sun beating down upon them.

Overwhelmed would best describe her state of mind as, one by one, the O'Briens introduced themselves. The siblings were the first to deliver greetings, beginning with Logan's sister, Mallory, and her husband, Whit, who had their four-month-old twin daughters with them, according to Logan. Then she met Aidan and his wife, Corri, followed by Kieran and his girlfriend, Claire. Devin introduced her to his "better half," Stacy, as little Sean tugged on Jenna's skirt and jabbered on about a puppy, as if they'd become fast friends. Lastly, Logan's parents took their turn.

"Jenna, this is my mother," Logan said as he planted his palm on Jenna's lower back, catching her off guard.

Obviously he was making certain she stayed steady on her feet, despite her cane. "It's nice to meet you, Mrs. O'Brien."

The woman took Jenna's offered hand into hers for a gentle shake. "It's a pleasure to meet you, too, Jenna. And, please, call me Lucy. We don't stand on formality here."

"And you can call me a pain in the arse." The booming voice hinted at an Irish brogue, and the hearty handshake told Jenna that the hulking figure standing before her was a man's man.

"Tell her your proper name, husband," Lucy scolded. "You'll have to excuse him, Jenna. After all the years we've been married, I've never been able to teach him any manners."

"I'm Dermot, Jenny."

"It's Jenna, Dad," Logan corrected.

"To me she will be Jenny. And she is the prettiest girl you've ever brought home to meet your old da."

Jenna's hand automatically went to her neck where a blush threatened. "Thank you, Dermot. I appreciate your hospitality."

She felt a nudge on her arm and recognized Logan's voice when he said, "Let's have a seat at the table before all the food's gone."

"Good advice, Logan," Dermot said. "The boys all eat like they've never seen food before, Jenny. If we're going to fatten you up, we might as well get a head start."

Jenna didn't have the desire to correct Dermot because she liked the fact he'd given her a pet name. She also didn't feel the need to "fatten up"; childbirth had added a few extra pounds she had yet to shed. But she was definitely hungry, for both good company and good food. She'd already received the first and, no doubt, would soon experience the second, if the delicious scent of barbecue wafting around her was any indication.

As they mingled with the various family members, Jenna acknowledged that joining Logan for the family get-together was proving to be a wonderful change of pace. She was glad she'd come, despite Logan's previous silence, something she chalked up to his surprise over her revelation. Amazingly he hadn't run in the opposite direction when she'd told him about her son. At least, not yet.

Maybe he was simply being a gentleman, and after today, they would part on good terms with a permanent goodbye. And that was just as well. Her life was much too complicated to entertain any ideas of pursuing a relationship with Logan O'Brien. Yet she couldn't help imagining what it would be like to do that very thing. What it would be like to know him on a much more personal level. Too many years had passed since she'd experienced intimacy with a man, and deep down she couldn't deny she'd missed that aspect of her life. Yet wishing for something that shouldn't be wasn't prudent, even if the thought was pleasant.

Logan showed her to what appeared to be a picnic table and helped her onto a bench, taking his place beside her. During the meal of smoked beef brisket and simple side dishes, everyone treated her as if she were a part of the family. Although, Lucy O'Brien had insisted on bringing her a plate of food—something she did for every guest, Logan assured her—no one had been the least bit condescending or overly concerned. The only indication that anyone even noticed her deficit came when Dermot asked, "What happened to your eyes, Jenny?"

"You're too nosy, old man," Lucy said.

Jenna pushed her plate back and folded her hands before her on the table. "It's okay, Lucy. I have a disease that's clouded my vision. And I hope to have it restored soon with corneal transplants."

"The miracle of modern medicine," Dermot replied. "I look forward to you being able to see what a handsome man I am."

The group shared in a laugh, including Jenna. Yet, it was Logan's laughter that had caught her attention. Logan who had kept her attention. Every now and then, her thigh touched his thigh, and even that simple contact brought about a certain amount of excitement and longing.

She'd sensed him watching her throughout the meal and wondered what he was thinking. If he leaned on the superficial side when it came to women, she would probably be outclassed. But if he preferred a more natural look, she might meet his expectations. Regardless, something about her had captured his notice, she decided, right before he declared, "You have barbecue sauce on your dress."

Great. He'd been analyzing an unsightly stain.

Embarrassed, Jenna lifted the paper napkin and asked, "Where is it?"

"In a place on your anatomy where I'm sure Logan would like to help you remove it."

"Shut up, Devin." Logan's tone was gruff yet hinted at humor. "Come inside with me and I'll take care of it."

"I bet you will, bro."

"That's enough, Kieran."

Jenna determined the time had come to make a quick exit, before the stain set in and Logan had to endure more ribbing. "I'd appreciate your help," she said as he clasped her arm and assisted her from the picnic bench.

"There's some white vinegar in the pantry, Logan," Lucy called while they headed back into the house. "Be sure to dilute it with cold water."

Once in the kitchen, Jenna leaned a hip against the counter while Logan noisily poked around in what she assumed was said pantry.

"I found it," he said, followed by the sound of running water. "Now I'm going to see if I can get this off."

Despite the warning, Jenna had a difficult time ignoring the steady swipes between her breasts, or the acrid scent of vinegar. "Lovely. Now I'm going to smell like a pickle."

"I like pickles." His smile shone through his

voice. "At least the spot looks better. Sorry about the cold water."

If he only knew how warm she'd grown during the stain-removal process. "I appreciate your efforts at eliminating the evidence of my clumsiness. But being blind has one distinct advantage. I can't see people staring at me when I'm wearing my lunch."

"They weren't staring at the stain," he said. "They were too busy looking at your black eye."

"I have a black eye? Sasha never mentioned it when she changed the bandage." Probably to save her from total mortification.

"Just a little bruising. The cut looks better, though."

"Did you tell anyone in your family what happened last night?"

"I told my brothers I picked you up in a bar after you engaged in a hair-pulling fight with a couple of coeds."

Oh, heavens. "You didn't!"

"We're hot-blooded Irishmen. We know all about bar fights."

"But I didn't engage in a bar fight, Logan."

"I'm kidding, Jenna. They didn't ask, and I didn't volunteer any information."

She playfully slapped at his arm. "Good, otherwise I'm sure your family will be glad when I leave, and hope I never come back." Oddly, she wouldn't mind coming back.

"My parents are very impressed with you, Jenna,

particularly my dad, who only gives a nickname to people he likes. The rest of the family is equally impressed. So am I, barbecue stain, black eye and all."

Considering their close proximity, Jenna was impressed she still maintained some semblance of composure. "Speaking of your family, I only counted three brothers. Who's missing?"

"Kevin, and he's probably off somewhere interviewing a high-paid baseball player for the magazine. He's never liked doing the family thing, and he hasn't come around much since Corri and Aidan got married."

"Why is that?"

"It's a long story, but the abbreviated version is Corri was engaged to Kevin first, and she ended up married to Aidan."

A soap-opera scenario was the last thing Jenna had envisioned. "She broke it off with Kevin to be with Aidan?"

"Kevin broke it off with her, and it was for the best. We all knew that, when Aidan kissed Corri in the kitchen before she and Kevin started dating, she'd picked the wrong brother."

"They kissed on the set where she does the cooking show?"

"Not the studio kitchen. This kitchen."

"Right here?" Her voice sounded a little strained.

"Right where we're standing." His voice

sounded much too sexy. "Have you ever been kissed in a kitchen, Jenna?"

"Not that I recall." But she had the strongest feeling she could very well get that kiss, especially when Logan formed his hand to her jaw and feathered his thumb over her cheek. A kiss she had secretly fantasized about since last night. She waited with an eagerness she couldn't contain. She braced herself for the impact of his lips on hers. She resisted the urge to shout "Go away!" when someone cleared their throat, halting any possibility of making her foolish fantasy a reality.

Logan took away his hand and asked, "What do you need, Kieran?" His impatience filtered out in his tone.

"Devin and Stacy are leaving to take Sean home for his nap. Mom thought you might want to say goodbye, if you're not too busy." He chuckled before the click of footsteps indicated his exit.

As much as Jenna wanted to see the couple off, she was in no shape to face anyone right now. "If you'll point me to the powder room, I'll be back outside in a minute."

"I can show you where it is," Logan said.

She raised her cane a few inches from the floor. "My trusty companion can help me find it while you say goodbye to your brother. Just tell me how many door handles and if it's left or right."

Without further protest, he took her by the shoulders and turned her around. "Straight ahead, second door on the right. Watch out for the curio cabinet in the hall to your left."

She greatly appreciated his confidence and trust that she could manage on her own, when so many people in her life insisted on treating her like an invalid. "I should be right out, but if I miss saying goodbye to Devin and Stacy, tell them I've enjoyed getting to know them better."

"I'll do that." She felt his presence immediately behind her and his warm breath at her ear. "And later, we'll work on getting to know each other better."

Fortunately Jenna had her cane to rely on, otherwise she might dissolve into the floor. She walked the hall on rubber legs while counting doorknobs. Using the cane to make certain the path was clear, she analyzed the sensual undertones in his words, and her physical response to them.

When she reached the room Logan had indicated, she found the door ajar and stepped inside. Now she could have a few moments alone to regain her composure and—

"Hi, Jenna."

She immediately recognized Mallory's voice. "I'm so sorry. I didn't realize you were in here."

"It's feeding time for the girls."

"You feed them in the bathroom?"

Mallory laughed softly. "You're not in the bathroom. This is my old bedroom, which has now been converted into a nursery."

Wonderful. Her transformation from bumbling barbecue eater to total idiot was now complete. "Logan told me the bathroom was the second door to the right."

"Logan must have forgotten to count the utility room. That's strange considering he's always been good at math."

Jenna assumed he was good at many things, the least of which was arithmetic. She pointed behind her. "I need to go one more door, then."

"Yes, but Corri's in there now, feeling the effects of morning sickness that continues all day."

"I didn't know Corri was pregnant."

"Oh, yes, and not feeling very well. You can go to the end of the hall and use the master bathroom if you'd like."

Jenna shook her head. "It's no emergency. I wanted to remove all the remnants of barbecue sauce in case it's on my chin as well as my dress." And splash a little water on her face to alleviate some of the heat.

"I don't see one drop anywhere, so keep me company while I nurse the girls. You'll find a chair about four steps in front of you."

Seeing the opportunity to question a woman who probably knew Logan better than most females, Jenna made her way to the chair and took a seat.

The soft suckling sounds sent a surge of longing through her, and the memory of unforgettable moments. "Do you feed both girls at once?"

"Rarely. Lucy's in the crib, playing with a newly discovered toy—her feet. She's the patient one. Madison is the chow hound and demands to eat immediately, or she throws a tantrum. But she falls asleep as soon as her belly's full."

Much the same as John David when he'd been a baby, and she'd still been able to care for him herself. "What do they look like?"

"They're identical. Both have Whit's dark hair and my green eyes."

"I'm sure they're beautiful." She instinctively suspected Mallory was, too, at least according to her husband who'd had no qualms about calling her "beautiful" several times during lunch.

"Would you do me a favor and hold Maddie while I feed Lucy? She's almost asleep."

Little did Mallory know, she was doing Jenna a favor by allowing her to cuddle a baby. "I'd love to."

The creak of a chair signified Mallory's approach right before her cloudy image came into Jenna's view. "I'm putting a burp pad on your shoulder, just in case," she said. "However, Maddie's not one to spit up, unlike Lucy. That's why I always give Lucy's burping duty to Whit."

Jenna smiled. "Husbands do come in handy at times, don't they?"

"Definitely. Whit's handy with a lot of things, which is how I got pregnant in the first place."

Jenna could relate on some level, although in the few months before the divorce, hers and David's lovemaking had been nonexistent. Yet, he had been good with J.D., and that had been her only priority at the time.

"Here she is," Mallory said as she laid the soft bundle in Jenna's arms.

Carefully Jenna lifted the baby to her shoulder and gently patted her back, once more filled with bittersweet recollections of good days gone by— the baby smells, the soft, soft skin, the beat of a tiny heart beneath her palm. "I'd forgotten how wonderful this feels," she said. "It's been a while since I've held a baby this small."

"I'd never held one this small before my nephew was born. I didn't babysit when I was younger, but fortunately Stacy let me practice with Sean."

"I never babysat, either." Aside from having no need to earn extra money, she'd never trusted her weakened eyes enough to take on that responsibility. "But I do have a son."

"Logan didn't mention that to us."

"Logan didn't know until today. John David doesn't live with me at the moment. He's in Tennessee with his father and his new stepmother for the next few months." Longer, if David had his way, even if Jenna did have the transplants.

"How old is he?" Mallory asked.

"Three and a half. He has to be watched closely these days, otherwise he's into something the minute you turn your back."

"Being away from him must be difficult for you. I barely make it through four hours of work before I'm dying to see the girls. Fortunately, my law firm has an on-site daycare and I'm only working part-time."

No one could know how very difficult it had been unless, like Mallory, they'd experienced motherhood. "J.D.'s father and I share joint custody, which was fine until he took the job out of state. Now I have to wait my turn to be with my baby. But I do talk to him every day." She sang him his favorite songs, told him silly stories, yet it still wasn't the same as tucking him into bed and kissing him good-night.

"How do you manage when he's with you?"

Jenna found Mallory's candor refreshing. "It isn't always easy, but it's doable, as long as I make sure there's someone else around." And that also had proven to be difficult, knowing she had to rely on a member of the staff to help her care for her own child.

A brief span of silence passed, interrupted by the steady rasp of the rocker moving back and forth. Jenna shifted little Madison into the cradle of her arms and made the decision to pose a few quetions while the opportunity existed. "What's Logan like?"

"Poor guy. He was hiding under the delivery table when they passed out the looks."

Not at all how she'd pictured him, even though it didn't matter. "I meant what's he like as a person? I've discovered that looks aren't as important as a man's character."

"Oh. First of all, I wasn't serious about the looks thing. In fact, I'd describe him as very handsome, but then I'm biased. As far as his character is concerned, he has a great personality, or he did have until…"

Mallory's faltering words caused Jenna a good deal of apprehension. "Until, what?"

"Until he hooked up with hellacious Helena Brennan, his onetime fiancée."

She recalled Logan mentioning the ex-girlfriend, but not in the context of a previous engagement. The first in what Jenna surmised would be a long list of surprising discoveries. "What happened?"

"Helena had more money than sense, and a devious side. She faked a pregnancy in order to trap him into marriage. Fortunately he discovered the truth on the eve of their wedding, before it was too late."

Jenna questioned whether Logan thought she'd done the same with David. In reality, she'd resisted the marriage until both he and her father had finally worn her down. "How long ago was this?"

"Almost a year. Since then, he's pretty much avoided any serious relationships, even if he hasn't necessarily avoided women. Logan's never been lacking for female companionship."

All the more reason why Jenna found it odd he would want to be with her. "I'm sure it's been hard for him to recover after being burned so badly, especially if he cared for the person doing the burning. I assume Logan did care for her."

"At the time it looked that way." Mallory sighed. "I never knew what he saw in Helena, but that's Logan in a nutshell—always seeing the good in people. He befriended kids in high school who were basically social outcasts and he took the shyest girl to the prom. That's what made him so popular with everyone."

And that could explain why he'd befriended her—poor blind Jenna. "That's a very honorable trait."

"Yes, it is, but if you're thinking that's why he's with you, think again. He might be benevolent, but in your case, he's infatuated."

What a ridiculous thing to assume. "We've known each other less than twenty-four hours. I promise he's not infatuated. He's only being nice to me."

"Yeah, right." When Mallory laughed, Lucy gave a little whine of protest. "Think what you will, Jenna, but I've seen the way he looks at you, like he's just discovered a new Corvette in the driveway. Trust me, he's definitely got a thing for you."

Since she couldn't see how Logan looked at her,

she'd have to take Mallory's word for it, although she had a hard time believing Logan's invitation today had involved anything but kindness. "Believe me, Mallory, Logan and I are only friends. There's nothing serious going on."

"So is this thing between you and Jenna serious?"

Logan continued to stare at the driveway that Devin and Stacy had left a few moments before. "I've just met her."

"Then your answer is no, it's not serious?"

He leveled a hard stare at his brother. "Are you intentionally being dense?"

Kieran grinned. "Nope. I'm just wondering why you looked like you wanted to jump her all during lunch."

"I sure as hell did not." Unfortunately, he sounded defensive enough to keep Kieran making more assumptions.

"Yeah, you did. And maybe you're not looking for a serious relationship, but you're seriously looking to get her into bed."

"Okay. I admit it. The thought's crossed my mind." More than once since he'd met her. "But that doesn't mean a damn thing, and I don't intend to act on it."

Kieran let go a loud laugh. "Sure, Logan. When you succeed in ignoring your animal urges, that'll be the day everyone in Houston carpools."

To hell with it. Kieran was on a tear and nothing Logan could say would change his mind. That meant the time had come for a change in subject. "By the way, where's Cindy?"

"We broke up six months ago."

"I didn't know that."

Kieran patted his back. "You've been too busy hanging out in bars and bedding hot babes to know what's been going on."

He refused to feel guilty over his absence from family dinners, even though he wasn't meeting much success. "Nothing wrong with playing a wide field. And I'm not looking for anything permanent."

"Neither am I, but sometimes things happen when you least expect it."

Logan had learned that hard lesson with Helena. "Just to set the record straight, as soon as I leave here, I'm taking Jenna to her house and saying goodbye. And that's going to be the end of it."

Chapter Five

"Do you have somewhere you have to be right now?"

Jenna looked as surprised by the query as Logan had been when he'd posed it. Regardless of what he'd said to Kieran earlier, he wasn't quite ready to let her go.

"As a matter of fact, I have plans," she said.

He pulled into the circular drive in front of the mansion and turned off the ignition. "With someone special?" Now, why in the hell had he asked that? And why had he sounded so jealous?

She grinned. "I thought I might join an Internet think tank and take a shot at solving global warming. Or maybe paint my nails, which is always challenging."

In spite of his chagrin, Logan couldn't stop his smile. "Good luck."

She shifted to face him. "I could be persuaded to put everything on hold. What do you have in mind?"

Several things, and kissing her topped the list. He'd halt that line of thinking right now if he knew what was good for him. Obviously, he didn't know what was good for him. "Nothing as monumental as the global-warming thing. I thought we could talk for a while."

"What time is it?"

He checked his watch. "Almost seven-thirty."

She frowned. "Darn. My father doesn't go to bed until eleven. I guess we could still go inside and take our chances that he doesn't sit us down and grill us on our day."

"I'm not afraid of Avery." Worried about their business relationship, yes. Afraid, no.

"He's not always gracious when it involves me and the opposite sex, Logan. He's basically interviewed every man I've ever been out with. That tends to put a damper on your social life, not that I've had much of one lately."

Logan's social life had been active—and empty. "We could have a drink somewhere."

She unsnapped her seat belt. "I have a better idea. A place I'd like you to see."

He almost asked if she meant her bedroom, but stopped short before the question shot out of his stupid mouth. "Where's that?"

"As soon as I get out of this monstrosity of a vehicle, I'll show you."

Logan barely made it to the passenger side right before Jenna attempted to exit on her own. Her stubborn streak was showing again, something he'd noticed back at his parents' house. Striving for independence seemed important to her, and he'd allowed her to find her own way all afternoon, while keeping an eye on her without her knowledge.

As they walked side by side, Jenna used the cane to navigate the flagstone path that led to the rear of the mansion. "Is the sun still out?" she asked.

"It's setting."

She pushed her shades up to the top of her head. "What color is the sky?"

"Blue."

"You can do better than that."

He had his doubts, but he'd try for her. "It has shades of orange mixed with the blue. And pink."

"See how much better everything looks when you notice the details?"

He'd never given the color of the sky much thought before now. And as far as details were concerned, he preferred to study those that involved her. She had a straight nose, full lips and golden highlights in her brown hair. Even without makeup, she was as beautiful—maybe even more so—than most of the women he'd known, both inside and out.

Damn. Twenty-four hours in her company, and she had him describing the sky and spouting poetry. He needed to hightail it out of there as soon as the opportunity presented itself. But what he wanted to do won out—stay a while longer—proving his common sense was in a headlock.

When they reached an ornate wrought iron gate, Jenna opened it with ease, indicating she'd been there before.

"This is my mother's garden," she said as they walked down a redbrick trail lined with various plants, marble statues and carefully trimmed hedges. "She designed the layout."

"My mom's into gardening, but her garden isn't as elaborate as this one." Just another reminder of their differing backgrounds.

"I've neve had much of a green thumb," Jenna said. "But I love flowers. Are we at the angel fountain, yet?"

Logan surveyed the immediate area and located the concrete landmark. "It's about ten feet ahead to the right."

Jenna picked up the pace, leaving Logan behind, and stopped before a bush covered in flowers.

"These are Gemini roses, although my mother referred to them as 'Jenna's roses' since I'm a Gemini." She bent over to smell one of the blooms. "That means you'll never know which side of me you'll encounter from one moment to the next."

So far, he liked all her sides, including her backside, which had his undivided attention at the moment. "Are you moody?"

She sent him a smile over one shoulder. "I prefer multifaceted to moody. Sometimes I'm into peace and serenity, other times I like adventure. Now, come here and get a closer look at these. They're beautiful."

"I'm really not into flowers."

Jenna carefully snapped one rose from the bush and faced him. "I never gave them much thought, either, before I couldn't see them any longer. There's a lot to be said for that old 'stop and smell the roses' adage." She stepped toward him and held up the flower. "Go ahead and take a whiff."

He swallowed his macho pride, circled her wrist and brought the bud to his nose. "Smells good."

She looked as if he'd presented her with a five-carat diamond. "Told you so."

She also looked like she wanted something else from him. He definitely knew what he wanted from her—the same thing he'd wanted from her back in the Hummer and back in his mother's kitchen, right before Kieran's untimely interruption.

After lowering her hand to his chest, he nudged her closer, trapping the rose between them. Her cane hit the ground with a clank.

He recognized she couldn't see him, but it almost seemed as if she could see right through him. For a brief moment he questioned his judgment and the possible cost of kissing her. But he'd be damned if he could stop when she whispered, "What are you waiting for, Logan?"

Suddenly, the area lit up like a baseball field, causing Jenna to flinch and close her lids against the harsh illumination.

He lowered her sunglasses back over her eyes, questioning if some cosmic force was in play—or her father. "Is this equivalent to your dad turning on the porch light?"

"They're security lights, set to automatically come on at dusk. I've always hated them. I hate them even more now."

After hearing the pain in her voice, he realized he needed to take her out of there. "You should probably go inside now."

"I probably should."

Logan retrieved the cane, placed it in her right hand and hooked her left arm through his. Silently they walked back to the house and stopped on the porch a few paces from the front door, where they remained in the shadows.

"I'm glad you invited me today, Logan."

So was he, more than he cared to express. "Everyone enjoyed having you there."

"I enjoyed them, too. In all honesty, I rarely have the opportunity to socialize these days, which is why I appreciate the invitation. You have a wonderful family."

"Some people find them overbearing." Including Helena, who'd reluctantly attended gatherings only when he'd insisted.

"They're refreshingly real."

He felt the same about her. Even though he couldn't predict where this thing between them might lead, he wanted to find out. "I want to see you again, Jenna."

She shook her head. "That's not a good idea, Logan. After a while, you'd begin to view me as a liability."

"That's bs, Jenna."

"No. It's true. I have a son, I can't see two inches in front of me and my father is your client."

"None of that matters."

"Believe me, it will eventually. I'd rather we part as friends." She held out her hand. "Again, thank you for a lovely afternoon."

Ignoring the gesture, he said, "I don't want to shake your hand."

"What do you want, Logan?"

"You know what I want, Jenna."

"To get into my pants?"

"They wouldn't fit."

"Ha-ha." She transferred her weight from one foot to the other. "I don't need to be rescued."

"I know that and—"

"I don't want a man making overtures because of some misplaced sense of chivalry. I'm not looking for—"

Logan pulled her into his arms and before some force of nature, or an overprotective father intervened, he kissed her—and not an innocent kiss by any definition.

Again her cane dropped to the ground as she draped her arms over his shoulders, while he bracketed her waist. He didn't hold back, didn't waste any time taking it to another level. He wanted to leave a lasting impression. He wanted to change her mind. And when she met the glide of his tongue with her own, he wanted to scoop her up, carry her off the porch and back to his condo.

Jenna pulled away and wrapped her arms tightly around her middle. "We can't do this, Logan."

"We already have and you wanted it as much as I did, Jenna. You asked me to do it in the garden."

"During a moment of weakness, and obviously, I had another of those a second ago."

So had he. "It was one helluva a kiss, and you know it."

She pointed at the ground. "Could you give me my cane, please?"

"That depends. Are you going to beat me over the head with it?"

Finally, she smiled. "No. But I should probably beat myself over the head with it."

"You've had enough head injuries for one weekend." He bent, picked up the cane, put it back in her hand and stroked his thumb across her wrist for good measure. "I'll be out of town on business for the next couple of days, but I'll call you later in the week."

"I'm not going to go out with you again, Logan."

When he heard the minimal conviction in her tone, he sensed that, with a little more effort, he might win this battle yet. "You might change your mind after you've had some time to think about that kiss."

She lifted her chin defiantly. "You've got a tremendous ego, Mr. O'Brien."

"You've got barbecue sauce on your dress, Ms. Fordyce. And the greatest smile, along with an obstinate streak as long as the interstate."

"Look who's talking. That's why it would never work between us."

"Oh, yeah, it would. And after that kiss, you should know how well it would work."

She clasped his hand and gave it a quick shake. "Again, thanks for lunch. Good night and goodbye."

Before he could respond, she'd entered the house and closed the door behind her, leaving him alone on the porch to evaluate the situation.

The blow to his pride had stung, but past experience had taught him when to push, and when to toss in the towel. It looked like it was towel-tossing time where Jenna Fordyce was concerned. Yet pride wasn't the only issue. Truth was, he liked everything about her, and that would be worth the effort to try and change her mind.

"I don't want you seeing him again, Jenna."

Using her cane to tap her way through the foyer, Jenna brushed past her father in search of the study. "We've already had this conversation, Dad. And you don't have to worry. After tonight, it's not going to be an issue."

"From what I witnessed happening between the two of you on the porch, I have reservations about that."

That sent her back around to face him. "You were spying on us?"

"I heard voices and I looked out the window. That doesn't constitute spying."

How she wished he would simply let her be a grown-up. "The only window in the vestibule flanks the door. That means you had to be standing at the door in order to hear the voices."

"What difference does it make?"

She braced both hands on top of the cane. "What I do and who I do it with isn't your concern."

"It concerns me when it involves Logan O'Brien."

His attitude was beyond logical. "For the past few years, I've only heard you say good things about Logan. Great things, in fact. To hear you tell it, he's God's gift to the business community. Highly intelligent, philanthropic, and the list goes on and on." Not to mention he had a very skilled mouth, an attribute she secretly added to the list.

"That was on a professional level, Jenna. This is personal. I've already told you he has a reputation—"

"I know. With women." After that kiss, she certainly could understand why. "And for your information, he treated me with courtesy. He also treated me like a normal person, a lesson a few people around here need to learn."

"I'm cautious because I care about you, sweetheart."

"I know that, Dad. And what happened between Logan and me, well, it was only a kiss."

It was one helluva kiss, and you know it...

She definitely knew it, even if she hadn't wanted to admit it to Logan, or to herself. "I'm going to call John David, then I'm going to bed. It's been a long day. Good night."

She saw the hazy movement before her, followed

by a brief kiss on her cheek. "I love you, sweet-heart," he said. "We'll talk about this later."

"I love you, too, Dad. And, no, we won't talk about it."

With that, she walked into the makeshift photo gallery and closed the door behind her before taking her favorite chair in the corner. She groped for the receiver on the end table and spoke the words "J.D." to set the dialer in motion. The phone rang three times before the familiar voice answered with a short, "Hello."

"Hi, David. It's me. Is John David still awake?"

"Ginger just gave him his bath. Let me see if he's out yet."

While Jenna waited to speak with her son, she tried to tamp down the envy over another woman bathing her baby. Another woman witnessing his milestones. Yet she'd understood when David had moved on with his life, even if it had meant bringing a spare spouse into the mix to serve as J.D.'s surrogate mother.

A clatter rang out in Jenna's ear right before the endearing voice said, "Hi, Mama."

"Hey, sweetie. Did you have a good bath?"

"Uh-huh. I played with a boat. Guess what, Mama?"

"What?"

"Daddy and Mommy Ginger are gonna take me on a boat. A big boat on the ocean."

Jenna swallowed hard around the unexpected news, and the fact he'd called David's new wife "Mommy." "When are you going on this boat, sweetie?"

"In the morning. That's why I gotta go to bed early."

She'd been literally left in the dark. "Do you want me to tell you a bedtime story or sing you our song first?"

"Not now, Mama. Daddy says we have to ride the airplane first to get to the boat so I gotta go to sleep. Can you come on the boat with me?"

If only she could. "Not this time, sweetie, but remember what I've always told you. Even if you can't see me, I'm always where?"

"In my heart."

"That's right, baby."

"I love you as big as the sky, Mama."

His willingness to recite their nightly routine eased her melancholy. "I love you as tall as the trees, sweetie."

"I love you as bright as the stars."

"I love you forever and ever."

"I'll put your picture in my suitcase, Mama. That way you can go on the boat with me."

The same picture she'd shown Logan earlier that day. The last picture they'd taken together.

She closed her eyes for a moment in an effort to fight back the threatening tears. "Have fun on the

boat, sweetie. Now, put your daddy on the phone."
She had a thing or two to say to him.

"Bye, Mama. Here's Daddy."

"I assume he told you about the cruise," David
said.

Her anger crept in again. "Yes, and you should
have told me, first."

"It was a spur of the moment thing, Jen.
Ginger's parents surprised us with the trip for
my birthday. I couldn't very well not accept until
I had your permission."

Jenna wasn't buying his excuses. "Your
birthday's in April, which means you've known
about this for two months. And the least you
could've done is discuss it with me."

"I've been busy."

"I call every night, David. You should have told
me the minute you knew."

"In all honesty, I didn't want you to have a lot of
time to obsess about the trip, which is why I didn't
mention it sooner."

Her anger arrived with the force of a gale. "I
wouldn't have obsessed over it."

"Yes, you would have. You worry about him
too much."

"He's my only child, David." The only child she
would probably ever have. "It's my right as his
mother to be concerned over his well-being and be
informed about his plans."

"You should've seen him, Jen. He was so excited when we told him this afternoon, he started packing immediately. Do you want me to tell him now that he can't go?"

To do so would be selfish on her part. "Of course not. I just worry—"

"I'll make sure he stays away from the railing, and we won't let him out of our sight."

He knew her too well. "Promise?"

"Promise. I have to go now and finish packing."

She wasn't ready to let him off the hook that easily. "How long will you be gone?"

"We fly to Florida in the morning and return next Sunday."

"You'll call me from the ship, right?"

"It's only a few days, Jen. I'll call the minute we return."

She couldn't tolerate not speaking to her child for that many days. "It's the least you can do, David. I only need him to call once. Since I can't be there, I'd like to know he's having a good time."

"He'll have a great time. We'll talk to you Sunday evening and he can tell you all about it then."

As much as she hated David's resistance, she couldn't very well force the issue. "Fine. I'll be waiting to hear from him. Give him a kiss for me, and please take good care of him, David."

"I will. Good night."

After hanging up the phone, Jenna released a litany of mild oaths and a few tears. She admittedly resented David's ability to give their child the adventure of a lifetime, while all she could offer was a nightly phone call. And all of her heart.

At times like these, she hated her deficit with a searing passion. Hated that she would be stuck for a whole week worrying about her son, and going to bed every night without hearing his voice.

She could only hope that, someday soon, she'd have her sight returned so her baby could be with her again. In the meantime, she'd do what she had to do to keep her mind off her troubles, although at the moment, she had no idea how she would fill all those lonely hours.

"How did the meeting in Kansas go, boss?"

Logan looked up from the paperwork he'd been staring at for over an hour to Bob, who was standing in his office doorway. "It went fine."

The man hitched up his pants beneath his big belly, strolled to the desk and pulled up a chair without an invitation. "So are you going to buy the planes?"

That still remained to be seen. He had enough assets to seal the deal, but he could use more capital. After building a successful business, he couldn't help but be ambivalent over letting go of his profits, and that's where his liaison with Avery Fordyce came in—if the man decided to cooperate. "I'll let you know as soon as I decide."

When Bob continued to study him, Logan lost what was left of his patience. "Anything else, Bob?"

"Just wondering what's got you so distracted."

A diminutive brunette. For the past two days, he hadn't been able to get Jenna out of his head, or his fantasies. "I'm not distracted, Bob. I'm tired. It's been a long two days."

"If you ask me, you could use a vacation. I don't remember the last time you've taken even a couple of days off."

Neither could Logan. "Right now that's not a priority."

Bob scrubbed a hand over the sparse hair on his scalp. "You know, boss, I learned a long time ago that you can burn the candle at both ends until you're burnt out."

He wasn't burnt out, at least, not yet. "Thanks for the suggestion. And, unless you have something business related to tell me, we both need to get back to work."

Bob pushed back the chair and stood, looking uncomfortable. "Someone's here to see you, but it's not business. It's personal."

Talking about beating around the bush. "And you're just now telling me that, Bob?"

"You might decide you're too busy for a visit."

Logan compiled a quick list of people he didn't care to see, and came up with two. One happened to be a client who always overstayed his welcome; the other was his former flame, and hell would ice before she'd show up at his office. "Tell me who it is, and I'll let you know if I'm available."

"Ms. Brennan."

The temperature just turned arctic in hell. "What does she want?"

"I didn't ask her, boss. She just said she needed a few minutes of your time and that it's important."

He couldn't imagine what Helena had to say, or if he even wanted to hear it. But he might as well get it over with because, knowing her, she'd force her way into his office. "Send her in, but tell her I only have ten minutes." The sooner he was rid of her, the better.

"Sure thing, Mr. O'Brien."

Before Logan had time to prepare, Helena Brennan strolled through his door, looking much the same as she had the last time he'd encountered her—the night he'd called off their wedding. She was a typical bombshell blonde—tall, long legs, great body and, at one time, he'd known every inch of it intimately. But today she wore a tailored white suit that wasn't up to her usual "got it, flaunt it" standards and her hair pulled back in a bun. In fact, she looked almost matronly.

"Hello, Logan." She paused too survey the

area. "You've redecorated your office." She ran her hand along the edge of the desk. "I like the chrome."

He didn't bother to respond or stand and that would send his mother into orbit. He did gesture toward the chair Bob had occupied a few minutes before. "Sit."

She complied and folded her hands primly in her lap. "I suppose I'm the last person you thought you'd see today."

She was the last person he wanted to see. "Why are you here?"

Helena flinched at his harsh tone. "I have something I need to tell you."

He knew exactly where this was heading. "Look, if you're wanting a reconciliation—"

"I'm here to tell you I'm getting married."

That he hadn't been expecting, and he couldn't deny the blow to his ego. "I would've read about it in the society page."

"It hasn't been officially announced yet, and I wanted you to hear it from me, first. I thought I owed you that much."

As if he really cared what she did or whom she did it with. "Who's the unlucky guy?"

"Randolph Morrison."

Old money uniting with old money. Figured. "Congratulations on the merger."

Anger flared in her blue eyes. "For your information, he loves me, although you might find that impossible to believe."

A year ago, he'd thought he'd been in love with her, too. "I hope the two of you have a long and prosperous life together." Prosperous was a given.

She shifted slightly in her seat. "In the year you and I have been apart, I've realized our relationship was destined to fail, and why."

"Was that before or after you pretended to be pregnant?"

Her gaze momentarily faltered. "I'm sorry for that. You know what they say. Desperate people do desperate things, and I was desperate to keep you. But I've changed, and I have you to thank for that."

He had a hard time believing that. "What do you mean?"

"You've opened my eyes to what I feel is important in a man, and I've found that with Randy. I now understand the reasons it didn't work with us, and it had as much to do with you as it did with me. Would you like to hear my conclusions for future relationship reference?"

He didn't want nor need her opinions. "Is this going to take long? I have a conference call in a few minutes." More like half an hour, but he wanted her out of there and out of his life for good.

She lifted a perfectly arched brow. "Are you afraid of taking a little constructive criticism, Logan?"

Like she had the right to criticize anyone. "If it makes you feel better, go ahead." •

"Good." She leaned forward and studied him long and hard. "You're a beautiful man, Logan, and you have a good heart. You're driven to succeed in business, almost too driven, but you're generous when it comes to strangers in need. You're a master at knocking the ground from beneath a woman's feet and getting her flat on her back in your bed using sexy, provocative words. And you also have the talent and skills to back them up. I know that better than anyone."

When she hesitated, Logan recognized the worst of the character assassination were yet to come. "But?"

"You have no idea how to be a friend to a woman."

His frame went rigid. "That sure as hell isn't true."

"Really? Then tell me my favorite color?"

Think fast, O'Brien. "Brown."

"Wrong."

"Is there a point to all of this, Helena?" Aside from citing his shortcomings.

She rose from the chair and clutched her purse in her arms. "The point is that if you ever become seriously involved with another woman, you might want to take her out to dinner a few times and get to know her, before you take her to bed. Ask her questions and let her know you're interested not only in her body, but in her mind, as well. You'd be surprised what a difference that makes."

She was seriously wrong. They'd been to dinner on numerous occasions during their time together. He'd taken her to several business functions, even if he had taken her to bed the first night they'd met. And the only thing on her mind when they'd dated had been the husband hunt…and shopping.

Logan saw no reason to rehash old recriminations. The past belonged in the past. "Your suggestions are duly noted," he said. "Anything else you want to rake me over the coals for?"

"Not at all, because I know that below your tough surface, there's a really great guy just waiting to come out and shine. It's going to take a very special woman to make that happen. I hope you find her soon."

She spun around and swayed out the door, giving Logan a glimpse of the Helena he'd known and had thought he'd loved.

He hated her harsh assessment. Despised that she viewed him as some shallow guy on the make who didn't give a damn about women. Hated that he'd found a measure of truth in her words, mainly when it came to the friendship part.

Fact was, he and Helena had never been friends. They'd had some good times and great sex, but beyond that, they'd shared little in common. She didn't like sports or his brothers. Going a week without a manicure was her idea of roughing it, and walking from the four-car garage into her father's mansion had been the only hiking she cared to do.

He doubted he would find the perfect mix of friendship and passion with a woman...unless he'd already found it in Jenna Fordyce. And that was a problem. Forming more than a casual relationship with her had several strikes against it—her father and that little issue of her refusing to see him again.

Maybe he could convince her to reconsider. Maybe he could prove to himself that he was capable of developing a solid friendship with a woman, even a woman who'd occupied his down and dirty dreams for three solid nights.

He could be setting himself up for failure if she refused to see him again, or even if she didn't. He wasn't sure how this would all come out in the end, but he'd be damned if he wasn't going try.

Chapter Six

When Jenna felt the shake on her shoulder, she pulled the headphones from her ears. "Yes, Sasha?"

"Sorry to be a bother, Miss, but you have a phone call."

For the past two days, she'd been counting the hours until she could reconnect with her son. She prayed David had reconsidered and the wait was finally over. "Is it John David?"

"No ma'am. It's a man."

Jenna's heart took a nosedive. "Does he have a name?"

"He said he's a friend, and that he enjoyed the roses."

She could only think of one man who might fit that description. "I'll take it." If only to hear a friendly voice. Anything to get her mind off her moping.

Sasha placed the phone in her hand and after Jenna heard the study door close, she answered with, "Are you looking for an invitation to see my garden again?"

"Not a bad idea, but it's fairly late."

As far as she was concerned, Logan's timing couldn't have been better. "I'm still wide-awake and probably will be most of the night."

"Why's that?"

"No offense, but I was expecting someone else, and I'm a little disappointed it wasn't him."

"You have another guy waiting in the wings, huh?"

Oddly, he sounded letdown. "Yes. A little guy. I haven't spoken with my son since Sunday. His father and new stepmother have taken him on a cruise."

"And you're missing him."

An accurate assessment from a man she barely knew. "You could say that."

"If you want some company, just say the word and I'll pick you up in a half hour. We could go for a drive or grab some coffee."

His persuasive voice served as an enticement, but good sense told her not to risk making a mistake when she felt so vulnerable. "I appreciate the suggestion, but—"

"Hang on a minute."

The line went silent for a few seconds until Logan came back to the phone. "That's a helluva lot better."

"What were you doing?"

"Undressing."

She had a detailed mental snapshot of that, even if she had no idea if it was accurate. "Do you make it a habit of taking off your clothes while you're on the phone with a woman?"

His laugh was incredibly seductive. "I'm not taking off all my clothes, just this damn noose around my neck and this stiff shirt. I only wear a suit and tie when I have to."

"The outdoorsman has spoken."

"Former outdoorsman. Lately I'm either trapped in my office or an airport."

She could relate to that, only, the house—and her vision loss—had led to her confinement. "I know what you mean. I really miss taking long walks. Fresh air and trees. I love pine trees."

"So do I. And I have an idea that's better than going for coffee tonight. We should go camping this weekend."

Jenna swallowed around her shock. "Are you serious?"

"Yeah. We could both use some time to get away. A trip between friends. There's an Arkansas state park in the Ozarks you'd enjoy."

She couldn't imagine accompanying him out

of state. In truth, she could, even though she shouldn't. "A friendly camping trip, huh?"

"Sure. No expectations. Just good company and conversation."

Jenna was very tempted to say yes but thought better of it. "Arkansas is fairly far way."

"We can leave on Friday and get a head start. If you'll go, I'll make the trip worth your while. I'm an expert camper."

She suspected his expertise went far beyond camping. "I suppose that entails pitching a more than adequate tent."

"Yeah, and with your help, I'll have it up in record time."

She couldn't disregard the suggestion in his tone, or her rather warm response to it. "Nothing like a confident camper. How are you at building fires?"

"Pretty good. I like to start out slowly, then stoke it until it's hot enough to melt steel."

She was veritably hot enough to melt steel. "What's your secret to that?"

"Good wood."

If she didn't stop this provocative conversation now, she'd agree to meet him tonight for a little fire building. Worse, she might agree to go away with him for the weekend. "Are you sure you don't expect more than a friendly trip?"

He sighed. "I'm sure, and I apologize for giving you the impression I expect more."

Quite a switch from the smooth sex talk he'd levied on her a moment before. Yet she wasn't certain she could trust him, or for that matter, trust herself. "Again, this sounds great, but I'm going to have to take a rain check. I need to be available in case John David needs me."

"He's miles away, Jenna, and I'm offering you a distraction."

He was already distracting her and presenting ideas she had no business considering. "With my poor eyesight, you'd have more of a burden with me tagging along than if you went alone." Or with another woman, and she was certain he had more than a few waiting in the proverbial wings.

"Come to think of it, you could be right. You might not enjoy the limited facilities. Not a masseuse or hair dresser within twenty miles. Just me, the wildlife and the fire."

He was wrong about her preferences. Dead wrong. "As I've told you before, I used to hike before my vision gave out on me. I'm very good at all the aforementioned camping aspects, I don't need to be pampered and I can handle a trail blindfolded."

"Then, prove it."

She hesitated a few moments, chastising herself for buckling beneath the power of his intentional baiting. Did she dare spend three days with him? Three days convening with nature, something she hadn't done in a long time. Three days outside the family mansion that had become her personal prison. Three days spent with a man who had seduction down to a science, regardless of his insistence he only wanted friendship.

"Okay. You're on." She only hoped she survived all his proficiency.

"Good. I'll pick you up bright and early Friday morning, and I'll have you home on Sunday in time to talk to your son."

She didn't do mornings very well. "How early?"

"It's a solid day's drive, so I'm thinking 5:00 a.m., unless you can't live without your beauty sleep, princess."

She made a note to put a large Thermos of coffee at the top of her list of things to bring, right beneath the speech she would write about the perils of calling her a princess. "I'll be ready."

"Great. One more thing—" he hesitated a moment "—I'm serious about being your friend, Jenna. I think we could both use that more than anything right now."

He certainly sounded sincere. "Can you really do that, Logan? Be only a friend to a woman without wanting anything else?"

"I'm going to give it my best shot, but I'll need your help."

In other words, she would have to try doubly hard to resist him if he failed to live up to his promise. Or maybe she wouldn't try to resist him. After all, celibacy wasn't what it was cracked up to be. They were both above the age of consent and, should the situation arise, she might decide to simply go for it while she had the chance. "One more thing. Which one of us is going to inform my father?"

"You just worry about packing, and I'll take care of Avery."

"Are you sure you want to do that, Logan?"

"Sure. How bad could it be?"

"If I were you, O'Brien, I'd turn right around and walk back out the door."

Logan had been threatened by fathers before, but none had been business colleagues. He could deal with Avery better if they were seated at a conference table, hammering out a deal not standing in the living room waiting for the man's daughter to appear so he could take her away. Even though Avery was wearing a blue robe instead of his usual silk suit, he looked formidable. He also looked like he could pick up the nearby fireplace poker and impale Logan with it if he didn't comply with his command.

Too bad. He wasn't going anywhere without Jenna. "Look, Avery, it's only for two days."

"Why are you doing this, Logan?"

He'd asked himself that same question several

times. The most important answer—he was on a mission to prove Helena wrong. And he'd been where Jenna was now—isolated from meaningful social interaction—only his isolation had been self-imposed. "Your daughter needs to do something other than sit around, waiting to hear from her kid."

"You don't have a clue what my daughter needs." He pointed at him and scowled. "And if you think I'm going to stand by and let you discard her as you've done countless women, you're sorely mistaken."

Logan should've known better than to frequent the same social events as Avery, a different escort in tow every time. "I don't intend to do that. We're only friends." Something he'd vowed to keep in mind this weekend. Granted, he wouldn't mind knowing her better in every sense, but he'd made the decision to adopt a hands-off policy, even if it might kill him in the process.

"If you truly have her best interests at heart," Avery said, "I see no reason why you can't take her to dinner in Houston instead of carting her thousands of miles away for some camping trip."

For the sake of civility and future business dealings, Logan kept a tight rein on his temper. "We're going to Arkansas, Avery, not Tahiti."

"I vote for Tahiti."

Both Logan and Avery turned at the same time to discover Jenna standing in the doorway, a black nylon bag slung over one shoulder, a cane that resembled a walking stick in her grip and a large black backpack resting at her feet.

"I hear Tahiti's crowded this time of year," Logan said, and then realized it sounded as if he wanted to get her alone—most likely the reason behind Avery's glare. Logan's lengthy appraisal of Jenna's midthigh khaki shorts, white sleeveless blouse and hiking boots probably hadn't helped. But the lethal combination of bare arms and bare legs—toned bare arms and legs for a woman of such small stature— meant only one thing. Big trouble. And if he didn't keep his eyes to himself, it could lead to his own demise—delivered at the hands of her father.

Avery moved to Jenna's side and wrapped his arm around her shoulder. "It's not too late to reconsider, sweetheart."

"I'm going, Dad. End of discussion."

Avery sported a serious frown. "I can't talk you out of this?"

She kissed his cheek. "You tried that last night, and nothing's changed."

He looked resigned. "Then, did you pack your allergy medication?"

"Yes, and my eyedrops, my toothbrush, clean underwear and bear repellant." She snapped her fingers. "Darn, I'm all out of bear repellant."

When Avery looked alarmed, Logan added, "We won't have to worry about that where we're going."

"Speaking of going," Jenna said, "shouldn't we be heading out before the traffic gets heavy?"

"Yeah, we should." Logan crossed the room and took her bags. "I'll meet you at the SUV as soon as I give Avery the contact information."

She smiled. "Sure. I'll expect you as soon as you reassure Mr. Fordyce that we're not running off to Vegas for a quickie wedding, or Tahiti. See you Sunday, Dad."

Cane in hand, she strode out of the room, leaving Logan alone with Avery, who nailed him with another hard glare. "I need to know where you'll be at all times."

With his free hand, Logan fished through his jeans' pocket, withdrew a piece of paper and handed it to Avery. "Here's the number of the campground and my cell phone, which you already have. Feel free to call in case of an emergency."

"Or in case we receive the call that corneas have become available," Avery said. "She'll have a limited window of time to return to Houston."

Logan hadn't stopped to consider the possibility of Jenna being unavailable for the transplant, and he was surprised she hadn't mentioned it. "If you get the call, I'll put her on a plane if I have to."

Avery forked a hand through his silver hair. "You have a lot to learn about Jenna, Logan. If you knew her, at all, you'd know that she hates to fly, particularly alone."

"I'll make note of that." And he would accompany her back to Texas in a chartered plane if necessary. "Speaking of planes, I met with the aviation company in Wichita on Monday. I can take delivery on the jets after the first of the year, if you're still willing to partner with me."

Avery rubbed a hand over his stubbled chin. "That depends. If you bring my daughter home unscathed, I'd be willing to back you financially. As long as you walk away from her afterward."

Logan knew the entrepreneur could be cutthroat, but he didn't realize he'd go to the extreme of using his daughter as a pawn. "We'll discuss it further next week."

"We'll definitely discuss it next week."

He didn't care for Avery's tone, or his suspicions. "You've always trusted me in business, Avery. You can trust me with Jenna."

He refused Logan's offer of a handshake. "My daughter is a very special woman. Remember that."

Avery Fordyce wasn't telling Logan anything he didn't already know.

Shortly after a fast-food lunch, Jenna drifted off to the drone of highway traffic, and had awakened a few moments before to the sound of crunching gravel. She stretched her legs and straightened in the seat. "Where are we?"

"In the Ozark National Forest."

Surely, she hadn't been asleep that long. "What time is it?"

"Almost four. We made it an hour earlier than I'd expected."

She laid her head back against the seat. "That's because we barely stopped since we grabbed the burgers."

"Did you know your lip trembles when you're asleep?"

Undoubtedly he'd been watching her. "I suppose you're going to tell me that I snore or, worse, drool."

"None of the above. But you did look like you were having a good dream."

Jenna didn't remember any dreams, although she did recall thinking about J.D. before she'd fallen asleep. She wondered where he was right now, if he was having a good time on the ship—without her. Of course, that would be her wish, even if she did experience some regret.

She had other things to think about to keep her mind occupied, and a question she'd been meaning to ask Logan. "Out of curiosity, exactly what did my father say to you before we left?"

"Not much, other than I'm supposed to deliver you safe and sound and unharmed on Sunday. In the meantime, I've been ordered to treat you with respect."

"He thinks you want to have sex with me."

Logan cleared his throat. "I'm here to be your friend."

"If I had to judge by the way you kissed me the other evening, and some of our conversation on Wednesday, I'd say you've thought about it."

"Okay, I won't deny that. But I've decided sex can complicate things, Jenna."

"That all depends on your mind-set."

"I guess so, if sex is all both parties want going into the relationship."

Spoken like the consummate player. Oddly, she hadn't viewed him that way since she'd known him, in spite of what her father had said. "If sex is only the primary goal, then it seems you're dealing with two callous people who don't give a damn about each other. And if that's the case, why would they want to have sex in the first place?"

"You just proved my point. You can't have sex with a friend without screwing up the friendship."

"You're saying that, in order for us to remain friends, we should avoid sex."

"Probably so."

Funny, he didn't sound that convinced. "I suppose you could be right." Or not.

"Your father would be glad to hear you say that."

"My father has nothing to do with my decisions, although, he's tried to intervene more than a few times in my life."

"That bad, huh?"

"You have no idea." She tilted her head back and sighed. "You've heard that old expression about running with scissors. He wouldn't let me run with a marshmallow. In fact, he didn't want me to run, at all."

"He only wants to protect you, Jenna."

"I know." She rested her hands loosely on her abdomen. "But he can't protect me from everything. Although, I understand why he's so bent on doing that."

"Like you've said, you're all he has."

"And it took my parents several years of trying to get pregnant before they finally adopted me."

"I didn't realize you were adopted."

Obviously, Logan and her father hadn't shared much when it came to their personal lives. "The adoption was final when I was six months old. Aside from that, I know nothing about my biological parents. It was a private adoption and the records are sealed."

"Have you asked your dad about them?"

"I did, not long after my mom died." That proved to be a disaster in the making. "I think he believed I was looking for a replacement for her. He was so upset, I didn't ask again until I was pregnant with John David. And once more, he was so distressed, I dropped it and haven't mentioned it since."

"But you wanted to know from a health care standpoint."

Another correct assumption. "At first, I wondered if she gave me up because she had the same disease I have. Later, I wanted to know what J.D.'s chances were of contracting it. He'll eventually be tested, but I'd like to be prepared."

"And if he does have it?"

She'd prayed night after night that wouldn't be the case. "Hopefully by the time he's my age, they'll have a cure."

They both fell silent for a few moments before Jenna added, "If my mother did give me up because she couldn't see, I wouldn't blame her at all. I'm sure she felt that it was the most unselfish thing to do."

"But you never considered that when you had your son."

"Not at all." She shifted to face him, wishing she could see enough to gauge his reaction. "I didn't worry about my future problems since John David has a father to help out. And even if I'd been on my own, I'm not sure I could have given him up. Maybe that makes me selfish, but it's hard enough knowing that another woman is practically raising him right now."

"I'm sure that is tough, but he still has you."

If only Jenna could believe she hadn't been replaced. If she could just be with him soon, touch him, hug him, tell him a bedtime story in person, not over the phone.

The conversation suspended for the time being, until Logan announced, "We're here," as he turned the SUV sharply to the right, braked hard and cut off the engine. "I'll be back in a minute."

Jenna didn't particularly like being left behind. "Where are you going?"

"To see what sites are available. The visitor center looks fairly crowded."

In other words, she might get lost among the masses. "Mind rolling down the window so I don't suffocate?"

"Sure."

Before Jenna could issue a protest, the door slammed, indicating Logan had left. She turned her face toward the open window and drew in the scents of pine, relished the warm summer sun and immediately fired off several sneezes.

She felt for the bag at her feet and withdrew her decongestants, along with the eyedrops. As much as she hated relying on medication, she hated runny noses and dry eyes even more.

After downing the pills with a sip of bottled water and applying the drops, she replaced the medicine and groped for the radio's controls. Nothing but static filtered through the speakers, which led her to believe they were far away from civilization, and that suited her fine.

The opening door indicated Logan's return. Or, at least, she hoped it was him and not some stranger.

He confirmed his identity when he said, "The place is packed, so we have two options."

Jenna hoped that turning around and going home wasn't one of them. "I'm listening."

"We can take the only spot left, but it's in the middle of the Falstaff reunion."

"I don't believe I know the Falstaffs."

"I met Billy Joe Falstaff while I was waiting in line. A nice guy. He offered me a beer and a date with his little sister, Liza."

For a second she wondered if Logan might take Billy Joe up on his offer after dealing with her deficits. Pushing the insecurity back where it belonged, she said, "How generous of him. What's the other option?"

"We can take the hiking trail that circles the valley. It's about fourteen miles all the way around, but there's several remote camping spots along the way."

She could live with remote. She preferred remote to a reunion of strangers. "That sounds like a good plan."

"The trail's pretty rough in places. Do you think you can handle it?"

"With your help, I can handle anything."

Chapter Seven

"Is this tether thing tying us together really necessary, Logan?"

As far as he was concerned, yes. "I didn't want you making a misstep when we reached the top of the bluff."

"Please tell me we're at the top of the bluff."

"We are."

"Good, because I feel like a dog and you're my handler."

If she only knew how much he wanted to handle her, she'd probably turn around and head back to Texas.

He regarded Jenna over one shoulder to see her

hair falling out of the band she'd secured at her crown, her cheeks dotted with dirt and a leaf hanging from her ponytail. She looked so damn cute, he wanted to kiss her. But he wasn't going to do it, otherwise he'd be breaking a promise, both to her and himself.

When he pulled up short, Jenna kept going and rammed into his back, face first. He turned and caught her by the shoulders to make sure she remained upright. "Whoa there."

She braced one hand on her hip. "Whoa? Now I've been relegated to pack mule."

Logan couldn't halt the laugh, which earned him a frown. "Stop complaining. I'm carrying a cooler, the tent and a backpack full of supplies."

"I'm not complaining, but I could use a drink and a break."

In reality, so could he. "Fine. We can rest for a few minutes, but we need to get down the hill before dark."

After he unhooked the tether from her belt loop, Jenna dropped her cane to the ground, pulled the backpack from her shoulders and set her other bag down before sitting beside them. She draped her arms on bent knees. "For a minute I thought we were going to walk all night."

He removed his gear, set it aside in a pile and stood above her. "I don't care what you say, you're definitely a princess, princess."

"I am not."

"Oh, yeah? Anyone who considers a foot massager their most prized possession is a princess."

She pulled a bottle of water from the side of the tote and took a swig. "Look who's talking. You're the one who can't live without access to twenty sports stations."

"That makes me a guy."

She picked up a twig and tossed it at his feet. "Shut up, Logan, or I'll short sheet your bed tonight."

"No beds available, just a blanket and the ground." Although he wouldn't mind a bed—with her in it. Naked.

Damn, he was a lost cause. But not yet. Thinking about it wasn't the same thing as acting on it.

After he heard a rustle in the nearby trees, Logan turned toward the sound. And when Jenna began to speak, he told her, "Be quiet and be still."

"If you say there's snake nearby, I'm going to—"

"Not a snake. A whitetail deer."

She came to her feet and brushed off her bottom. "Where is it?"

"In a clearing to your left, about fifty yards or so. It's heading this way."

She knelt, carefully opened the backpack and withdrew a digital camera. "I want a picture."

A photographer he was not. "I'll try, but I make no guarantees on quality."

"I'm going to help you," she said in a whisper.

"Come here and stand behind me. You point and I'll shoot."

He saw no reason to protest. In fact, he'd damn sure enjoy standing behind her. With that in mind, he positioned himself at her back and turned her in the direction of the wildlife. "What do I do now?"

"First of all, describe the deer."

"You've never seen one before?"

"Of course I've seen one. I just want to know what this one looks like."

Logan studied the animal foraging in the grass while inching closer, oblivious to their presence. "It's brown, with a white tail." He saw another flash of tan in the distance. "It's a doe. She has a fawn with her."

"Baby animals make great subjects," she said. "Let's hurry and get a picture before they run away."

Logan moved flush against her and ran his palms down her arms before lifting the camera to his eyes. "It's focused." And he was quickly in danger of forgetting his friendship goal. But he couldn't very well help her with the picture if he didn't touch her.

"Now, keep looking through the lens," she said. "And keep the camera steady. I'll do the rest."

He wasn't sure he could trust himself to keep the camera steady with her so close.

"Are you ready?" she asked.

Oh, yeah. Real ready, but not necessarily in a photography sense. "Shoot."

She set off the shutter in rapid-fire succession right before the deer bolted and took off in the opposite direction.

"They're out of here," Logan said as he gave the camera back to Jenna with one hand while keeping his other resting loosely at her waist. He should back away from her immediately, but his feet didn't want to move, and his hand had developed a will of its own.

"Feel free to let go of me now," she said.

Apparently she could read his mind, and letting her go was the last thing he wanted to do, but he did. Reluctantly.

While he returned to the nylon cooler and crouched to retrieve a sports drink, Jenna wandered to the opposite side of the trail.

"Be careful," he told her as she took a few steps toward the edge of the bluff. "You've got a drop off about fifteen feet in front of you."

"What does the scenery look like?" she asked.

"There's a valley below and a creek. And mountains covered with trees in the distance."

"I'm going to take a few more pictures, then we can be on our way."

"Do you need any help?" He sounded way too eager.

"Not this time. I'm going to rely on my intuition."

Drink in hand, Logan straightened and kept a

close eye on her. So far so good, he thought as she remained in the same spot, snapping pictures nonstop.

But when she started forward, every instinct he owned screamed danger. He tossed aside the bottle and caught her with one arm around her middle, impeding her progress.

As he carried her back to the trail, his chest constricted around his hammering heart. "Dammit, Jenna, I told you to be careful," he said as he set her down without letting her go.

She sent him a sour look. "You said fifteen feet. I only moved two."

Hardheaded woman. "If you'd kept going, you would've walked right over the edge."

"Do you really think I'm that stupid?"

"I think you take chances you don't need to take."

She wrested out of his hold. "Thanks for the vote of confidence, Logan. Are you proud of yourself now?"

"I don't know what in the hell you're talking about."

She draped the camera's strap around her neck. "You've done your good deed for the day, saving a distressed damsel whom you believe doesn't have the sense of a pack mule. Isn't that what this is all about between you and me? Your need to come to the rescue of a helpless, blind woman?"

"You're about as helpless as a fully armed militia."

"And you want to serve as my guardian. I don't need a guardian, Logan."

He only needed one thing from her at the moment, right or wrong. "As far as you and me are concerned, this is what it's all about."

He kissed her hard, and deep, driven by adrenaline and anger. Maybe even some latent fear.

He expected her to pull away and slug him, but so far she hadn't done one thing he'd expected. Instead, she willingly participated in the kiss, and in many ways took the lead. She rubbed her hands up and down his back. He pulled her closer. She executed a full body press against him. He inched his hands beneath the back of her shirt.

He had half a mind to take her down on the dusty ground just to feel her beneath him. The other half of his mind, located below his skull—not his belt—told him that wouldn't be at all comfortable for her.

He had a blanket nearby and a large expanse of grass at his disposal. If she wanted a longer break, he'd be glad to oblige her. If she wanted to know just how badly he wanted her, he'd be more than happy to show her. And if he wanted to retain some honor, he'd stop the thoughts and the mouth action immediately. A tough decision, particularly when she acted as though she didn't want him to stop.

Something brushed Logan's leg, forcing him to break the kiss. He looked to his left to see a patch of black loping away.

"Was that another deer?" Jenna asked.

"I think it was a Labrador retriever."

A whistle sounded, followed by a feminine voice calling, "Get back here, Perry."

So much for being alone. So much for his plans to engage Jenna in a heavy make-out session. And that was just as well. If he'd let his libido do the talking, they wouldn't have made it to the campsite until well after dark—and he might have made a fatal error in judgment. Not a good thing to do if he wanted to befriend her, even if he also wanted to bed her.

After nudging Jenna aside, Logan snatched her cane from the ground and handed it to her. "Time to hit the road again, princess."

"If you don't stop that princess stuff, I will find a way to pay you back."

He leaned close to her ear and said, "You already have. Right now I'm in a helluva lot of pain, thanks to you."

Her mouth gaped open momentarily. The sunglasses prevented him from seeing her eyes, but he figured she had that whole "shooting daggers" thing going on. "Thanks to me? You kissed me first, *friend.*"

Like he'd really forget that. "You didn't stop me, did you?"

She shook her head. "This is ridiculous. I'm not the type to lose control because some guy has a way with his tongue."

"I'm not some guy, Jenna." And she wasn't just any woman, either.

"Whatever." She flipped her hand in dismissal before gathering her equipment from the ground, but he would bet his last limo that she was as unable to ignore their attraction as he was.

Logan had a strong feeling only time would tell how long he could keep his distance before only friendship went the way of the wind.

As they lay side by side on their backs on a blanket, bedrolls supporting their heads, Logan noticed that the fire he'd built earlier had cast Jenna's profile in a golden glow. Since dinner, he'd noticed a lot of things about her, including her ability to avoid certain subjects, namely what had happened on the trail earlier in the day, and the fact that, at some point, they had to climb into the tent together.

Jenna released a satisfied sigh, disturbing the quiet. "Summer's my favorite season. I wouldn't mind if we had hot weather year-round."

He wouldn't mind if someone would douse him with a bucket of ice water, otherwise he could be in for a long, hard night. "That's a good thing since we live in Texas."

"True." She stretched her arms above her head and dropped them at her sides. "When I was little, I used to go outdoors late at night, lie on the ground and watch the stars. Sometimes I'd fall asleep until morning and I'd have to sneak back in before my parents caught me."

"You were daring even as a kid."

"Yes, I was. Fortunately I've never been afraid of the dark, otherwise I'd be in serious trouble now."

Occasionally she would slip in a reminder of her blindness, and Logan didn't know if that was for her benefit, or his. "During the summer, I'd stay up late and play basketball with my brothers until the neighbors complained."

"And your parents didn't object?" She sounded in awe of that concept.

"No. Probably because they were glad to get us out of the house."

"That must have been wonderful, having siblings. I only had myself to talk to at home. After a while, that gets rather boring."

Logan had five siblings he had to talk over in order to get a word in edgewise. "It had its ups and downs, particularly when we'd get into fights."

"You didn't really hurt each other, did you?"

"I suffered a few black eyes in my time. We were more afraid of what my father would do after he broke them up."

"Were you afraid of anything else when you were a child?"

The question took him by surprise. "Not that I can think of."

She touched his arm. "Come on, Logan. Everyone has fears. I promise I won't tell anyone and destroy your rep as a tough guy."

He'd never been into soul baring, but for some strange reason, he didn't feel the need to hold back with Jenna. "For a long time, I used to be afraid of heights before I forced myself to get over it. That started after Aidan pushed me out of the top bunk bed when I was about five and I landed on my face. I had to have stitches."

"Where?"

"On my chin."

She reached out and ran a fingertip along his face, sketching a path beneath his bottom lip. "Right here I feel a scar. Nothing big, but it's there. I'm surprised I missed it before."

He was surprised by his reaction to only a simple touch. "I was lucky I didn't lose any teeth." He would be lucky if he didn't lose his cool when her palm came to rest on his abdomen. "What about you?" he asked. "What were you afraid of when you were a kid?"

"Honestly, not much. Adulthood is another story altogether."

He could think of several fears she might have

and he wanted to know them all. "What are you afraid of now, Jenna?"

"Snakes."

"Seriously."

"I am serious. Oh, and I don't like crowded elevators."

"Is that it?"

She shifted onto her back and broke all contact between them. "I'm afraid my son will forget me."

The abject sadness in her voice cut Logan to the core. He'd never been all that good at consolation, particularly when it involved women. For her, he would try.

After taking her hand, he placed it on his chest. "I doubt your son will ever forget you." He'd never forget her, even if this weekend was all they would ever have.

She worked her way into a sitting position and said, "Enough of that. We're here to have a good time, not to discuss the past or worry about the future."

She'd said it with a good deal of bravado, but Logan surmised she did so only to cover her emotional scars.

When she tried to hide a yawn behind her hand, he said, "Looks like the good times will have to start over in the morning. I have the tent up if you're ready to get some sleep." A tent barely big enough for both of them. A test of his willpower.

She pushed off the blanket and came to her feet. "It's too hot to sleep."

He'd have to agree, especially when she began to unbutton her blouse. "If you want some privacy, I can take a walk."

She slid the blouse away. "I want to go for a swim in the creek and wash the grime off my body."

He wanted to tackle her where she stood. "Did you bring a suit?"

"I don't need one."

Oh, hell. "You're going to go for a midnight swim in a state park, buck naked?"

"What's a little nudity between friends?"

To a man who was really trying to behave, a lot. "We're not the only people around here."

"I haven't seen a soul, but if it makes you feel better, I'll leave my underwear on." She dropped the blouse on his lap, concealing the first signs of an erection that fortunately she couldn't see. "And you're going with me."

He rubbed a hand over the back of his neck and tried to avert his gaze, without success. "It's too dangerous, Jenna."

She looked highly frustrated. "You told me earlier today the creek's not deep at all."

"Me and you swimming together, with you in your underwear. That's dangerous."

"Surely, you've seen a woman dressed only in a bra and panties before, Logan."

He hadn't seen her that way before—until now.

She shimmied out of her shorts, leaving her wearing only a skimpy white bra and skimpy white panties, setting a sufficient trap for Logan's hyped-up hormones. "Are you trying to test me, Jenna?" If so, he was failing.

She pulled the band from the top of her head and shook out her hair. "I'm trying to cool off."

And in the process, heating him up to bonfire intensity. "I didn't bring a suit, either."

"Then feel free to strip down to your drawers. Better still, get totally naked. I'll never know."

Yeah, she would, if he got anywhere near her. "That's probably not a good idea."

"It's a great idea." She hovered above him, one hand fisted on her waist. "Get up, O'Brien."

He already was. "Are you sure you want to do this?"

"Positive."

What the hell? Like she'd said, she couldn't see him, but that didn't change the fact he could see her. A lot of her, from the outline of her breasts to the minimal strip of fabric between her thighs, and all notable parts in between. At least, until they got into the water.

As he tugged the T-shirt over his head and snaked out of his jeans, he made a firm commitment to keep his hands to himself. Maybe he should tie them both behind his back.

* * *

Jenna stepped into the creek and immediately experienced the heady rush of freedom. She curled her toes into the sandy bottom as water lapped at her ankles. Cool water that reminded her of her companion. Although Logan had a firm grip on her hand, he didn't say a word, and she suspected he was literally keeping her at arm's length.

She couldn't exactly fault him. After all, he seemed to be struggling with control, and she had only herself to thank for that. She'd welcomed his kiss earlier in the day. She'd invited him for a swim without the benefit of clothes. And she'd known exactly what she was doing.

All the talk of friendship, of no expectations, had dissolved with every passing moment. With each and every kiss. Some might not understand why she would take such a risk with a man she didn't know that well. Frankly, she didn't care. Didn't care what her father might think or what anyone would think, for that matter. She had a very virile male at her disposal, and she planned to take supreme advantage of the circumstance.

"We're only going to go a little farther," Logan said, breaking into her thoughts.

That remained to be seen, as far as Jenna was concerned, though she recognized he'd been referring to their swim.

After the stream encircled her midriff, Jenna

wrested from Logan's grasp and plunged beneath the surface, a watery cocoon where she could wash away the dust and the last of her concerns. The night sounds gave way to serene silence and complete darkness, yet, she wasn't afraid at all. Not when a beautiful man waited for her.

After a few moments, Jenna came up for air and slicked back her hair with both hands. "This feels wonderful." When she received no response, she questioned if she'd finally driven him away with her daring. "Logan?"

"I'm still here."

Of course he was still there. He wasn't the type to leave her to her own devices; he'd demonstrated that when she'd gotten to close to the edge of the cliff. She felt as if she were teetering on another edge right now, looking for a safe place to land. Her instincts told her Logan was that safe place, at least, temporarily, as long as she kept her emotional wits about her.

"Where are you?" she asked.

"To your left." He caught her hand beneath the water and urged her closer.

Her curiosity beckoning, she moved behind him, using his shoulders for support. His skin was damp and taut, she realized as she investigated his back, tracing a line with a fingertip down his spine until she contacted the rise below his waist. Wisdom warranted she halt the examination, but she wasn't feeling very wise at the moment. She was feeling somewhat restless and warm. And she had to know exactly what he was wearing—or not wearing.

Jenna received her answer when she splayed both her palms over the sides of his hips. His bare hips. Aside from a slight tremor, he remained very still as she explored the curve of his well-defined bottom.

"Nice butt, O'Brien."

He clasped her wrists and pulled her around in front of him. "I'm warning you, Jenna." He sounded stern, but not so intimidating that Jenna would veer from her goal.

"Consider me sufficiently warned," she said. And amply excited.

"Do you realize what you're doing?"

"I'm finding out for myself what all the ladies see in you."

"You're stirring up trouble."

"How much trouble?"

He tugged her forward and pressed his pelvis against her. "Does that answer your question?"

Yes, it had. He'd verified he was patently male, and that he had impressive attributes any women would find appealing. Most important, he'd proven that he wanted her, at least, in a physical sense. And she wanted him.

She decided to go for broke. To go for it all. On that thought, Jenna reached behind her, unclasped her bra and tossed it in the direction of the bank. In order to remove her panties, she'd have to rely on Logan's assistance and opted to let him do the honors later.

She slid her hands up his chest and toyed with the fringe of hair at his nape. "Now we're almost even."

She then became the aggressor, and kissed him first.

When he released a feral groan, Jenna recognized she'd sufficiently unleashed something in him, spurring an all-out sensual attack on her mouth. She was mildly aware of a waterfall gurgling in the distance, the hum of locusts and the trill of a bird. She was more aware of Logan's touch on her bottom, then on her breasts.

Too many lonely months had passed since she'd felt so alive, so in tune with her body's need. She craved the intimacy that he could give her, and fought frustration when he took his hands away.

"We've got to stop this," he muttered. "Before I can't stop."

"I've decided to remove *stop* from my vocabulary."

Her attempt at levity fell flat when he said, "I'm serious, Jenna."

"So am I, Logan."

"What about our friendship pact?"

"We'll be really close friends." Yet, she had one serious concern she needed to voice. "When we talked about our fears earlier, there's one I'd failed to mention. Unplanned pregnancy."

"That's only one reason why this isn't a good idea. I didn't bring any condoms."

Major warning bells rang out in her head. "Do you make a habit of not being prepared when you're with a woman?"

"I'm always prepared, just not this time."

Her confidence cracked, sending her back a step. "Then I must have assumed wrong. I thought you wanted me as much as I wanted you."

He brought her back into his arms. "You know damn well I've wanted you since the night we met. I didn't pack condoms because I worried your dad might search my gear. I also didn't want to be tempted to go back on my word."

He'd picked a fine time to be noble. "This definitely presents a problem."

"Yeah, it does." His voice held a world of disappointment, bolstering Jenna's determination.

She saw no reason to end a perfectly good evening on a sour note. "You might not understand this, Logan, but I wake up every morning alone, and I go to bed alone. Sometimes the craving for a human touch is so strong, I ache. Tonight, I'm asking you to give me that much, even if it means we're only going to hold each other."

"It's going to be tough to leave it at that, Jenna."

She brushed a kiss over his cheek. "I know it will

be. But I also know you're strong enough to deal
with it."

"I'll try."

"That's all I'm asking of you." At least, for the
time being.

Chapter Eight

"Did you know that in every square inch of skin, there are over a thousand nerve endings?"

Logan was aware of every one of them at the moment. "No, I didn't know that."

He did know that he was back on the blanket near the fire he'd rekindled, covered only by a thin sheet and a pair of boxers, an incredible, half-naked woman curled against his side—and they'd done nothing more than talk for the past half hour. None of his brothers would believe this. *He* didn't believe it.

Jenna lifted his hand and gave his fingers a flex test. "Did you know that over thirteen hundred nerve endings exist in one fingertip alone?"

And he could think of at least that many reasons why he should put her in the tent while he slept outside tonight. But leaving was the last thing on his mind when he rolled to his side to face her, bringing him up close and personal to her bare breasts. "You must've enjoyed your anatomy classes in college to have retained all that information." And he really didn't need an anatomy lesson. His own anatomy was giving him enough problems as it was.

"I didn't come by the information in college." She flipped her hair back from one shoulder, a feminine form of enticement that Logan recognized immediately. "When I realized it was inevitable that I'd eventually lose my sight, I started studying the optic nerve, which led to the discovery of neurons and receptors, specifically those involving touch. Now, close your eyes and lie back so you can get the full effect of my research."

"I like looking at you." He also worried he might not endure her research without having a lapse in judgment.

"I promise you'll enjoy it."

Exactly what he feared. "Does it mean that much to you?"

"Yes, it does. I want you to experience what I do without the benefit of sight. And don't cheat just because I can't tell whether you have them closed."

"Fine. Be careful or you'll stir up more trouble."

He'd only recently recovered from the effects of their swim and her insistence on remaining topless.

After he shut his eyes and shifted onto his back, Jenna whispered, "I've learned that several areas are very sensitive, such as the face." She kissed him on the forehead, the cheek and the chin. "So are the back of the neck and upper arms." She massaged his nape before raking her nails lightly over the bend of his shoulder and down his biceps. "And the chest." She pressed her lips against his sternum, not once, but twice. "Of course, the area between the legs is very sensitive."

Thankfully, she didn't go there, otherwise he'd be saluting the entire campground. "Interesting."

"There's more."

Logan wasn't certain he could stand much more. "Can you give me hint so I'll be prepared?"

"You'll have to wait and see."

Even with his lids closed, he was all too aware she'd moved partially on top of him and very aware of her breasts rubbing against his chest. As much as he wanted to touch her, he kept his hands balled at his sides and waited for what would come next.

"Receptors known as Krause corpuscles respond to pressure," she said. "They're located in the lips and on the tongue."

She did exactly what he'd expected, and wanted her to do—kissed him. She also demonstrated exactly how much pressure on his tongue it took before he was tempted to turn her over and plunge inside her. Luckily, she pulled away just in time for him to get his grip on the last of his control.

"You'll also find those same receptors a little lower." When she streamed her hand down his abdomen and traced the path of hair below his navel, he opened his eyes and caught her wrist. He brought her hand back to his chest right before she could reach beneath his shorts to discover the rock-hard land of no return. "Don't do it, Jenna. I've been able to handle your little seminar to this point, but if you keep this up, I'm going to lose it."

He couldn't completely make out her expression in the limited light, but he did see a flash of white teeth, indicating she was smiling. "That's the idea."

In one smooth moved, he flipped her over onto her back and raised her arms above her head. "I'm only so strong, Jenna."

"But the only way I can see you is through touch, and I have to see you." She threaded her fingers through his hair and sighed. "It's been so long since I've had any intimacy with a man, Logan. I just want…" She covered her face with her hands. "Maybe I don't know what I want."

But Logan recognized what she needed, and he'd gladly give it to her. "Do you know what I see when I look at you?"

She attempted a half-hearted smile. "A desperate woman?"

He ran his finger down the column of her throat. "A beautiful woman."

"I don't know about that."

He pressed a fingertip against her lips. "Don't speak, Jenna. Just listen."

He guided his palms down her rib cage and back up again, coming closer and closer to her breasts with each stroke. "You have a great body, and right now I want to do things to you that you won't forget."

You're a master at knocking the ground from beneath a woman's feet and getting her flat on her back in your bed using sexy, provocative words....

Ignoring Helena's intrusion into his brain, he outlined Jenna's nipples with a fingertip. "I want to use my hands and my mouth on you."

Her bottom lip trembled. "Where?"

"Everywhere."

...you also have the talent and skills to back them up.

He toyed with the lacy band below her navel. "I want to hear you beg for more, Jenna. And I want to give you more."

...let her know you're interested not only in her body, but in her mind, as well. You'd be surprised what a difference that makes....

Damn Helena for dropping into his mind at an inopportune moment and for making sense.

Logan planted his palms on either side of Jenna

and lowered his head. "And as much as I want to do all those things to you, I can't."

She looked totally dejected. "Why not?"

He straightened and sat beside her, arms draped on his knees. "It has to do with something some-one told me."

"Excuse me?"

"Someone I used to know."

"I'm glad you're referring to a real person. For a minute I thought you were hearing voices."

He had heard only one voice—Helena's—and he wished he could shut it up. "She surprised me with a visit."

"She?"

"My former girlfriend."

"You mean your former fiancée, Helena, don't you?"

He centered his gaze on Jenna to find she'd thankfully pulled the sheet over her breasts. "How did you know about her?"

She folded the cotton edge back and forth. "Mallory mentioned her last Sunday. She told me the circumstances behind why you called off the wedding."

Leave it to Mallory to air his business. "And I haven't seen Helena since, until she showed up at my office three days ago."

"I see. You're getting back together with her and I was your last hurrah until your conscience intruded."

He could understand why she might think that, even if it was an erroneous assumption. "She stopped by to tell me she's getting married."

"Oh. That's good." She sounded and looked relieved.

Logan reclaimed his spot beside Jenna, stacked his hands behind his head and stared at the sky. "She also said a few things about me that I didn't particularly like. But she's right."

When Logan turned his head to gauge her reaction, Jenna rolled onto her side and propped her cheek on her palm. "What sort of things?"

As difficult as it was to tell her the truth, she deserved that much. "She told me I have the seduction technique down pat, but I don't know how to be a good friend to a woman."

"And you believe her?"

"I didn't want to, but it's true. I've had my fair share of lovers, but not any female friends to speak of."

"I don't agree." She snuggled up against his side and laid an arm across his chest. "Since the night we met, I've considered you a friend. Someone who was willing to take off my mascara and not my clothes. Someone who took me home only to make sure I was safe. And most important, someone who brought me to this wonderful place where I feel totally liberated for the first time in years."

He grinned. "Someone who still wants to jump your bones."

She returned his smile. "I'm so happy to hear that. I thought perhaps my receptor recitation was a huge turnoff."

"It was sexy as hell." He lifted her hand and kissed it before sitting up again. "But right now we're going to go inside the tent and we're going to sleep together, literally."

"Then, you're saying we're going to keep our relationship strictly platonic?"

"I'm saying we're going to take it slow, for now."

"For as long as we're here?"

"For as long as it takes to know each other better." After wrapping her up in the sheet, Logan stood and pulled her into his arms. "First, you're going to put your clothes on, otherwise I might be tempted to get too friendly."

"Can you handle a little sociable spooning?"

Another test of his will, but something that she needed. For that reason, he'd accommodate her. "You bet. And before we go to bed, I want to let you in on a few things I've learned about you. Good things."

She smiled. "I know a great male butt when I feel it?"

He appreciated her attempt at humor, but what he had to say was serious business, particularly for a man who wasn't always good at expressing himself outside the realm of sex. "You know who you are, you know what you want out of life, and you're determined to get it. You have a killer body, but your strength, Jenna Fordyce, is the most attractive part about you."

She rested her cheek against his shoulder. "I don't always know who I am, Logan, and I'm not always that strong. But I do know I'm thankful that, for the first time in a very long time, I won't have to wake up alone."

The following morning, Jenna awoke to the smell of fresh coffee and a soft kiss on the cheek, delivered by a man who had put honor above all else last night. As much as she'd appreciated his resolve to take it slowly, it still didn't change her decision to have a more intimate relationship with him before the end of the weekend. Before the end of the day, if she had her druthers.

"Did you sleep okay?" Logan asked in a very tempting, very grainy voice.

She stretched her legs and tried to focus on the figure beside her, to no avail. She ached to see him in the light of day, and imagined how he might look. Tousled hair. Unshaven face. Bare chest. Her favorite combination.

Jenna reached for his arm to discover he'd put on a T-shirt, ran her fingers through his thick hair and touched his scratchy chin; her only means of confirmation. "I slept great." And she had, in his arms. "How about you?"

"I was up earlier than I'd planned to be, thanks to Perry. I'm surprised you didn't hear him barking."

"I vaguely remember that, but I was too tired to pay any attention."

"He returned this."

After Logan pressed a ball of damp fabric in her palm, a moment passed before Jenna recognized what she was holding. Lovely. "It's my bra."

"Yeah. He must have found it on the bank where we left it last night."

"Once a retriever, always a retriever."

Logan's ensuing laugh served as morning music to Jenna's ears. "True. After his wake-up call, I couldn't go back to sleep, so I built a fire and made coffee."

An extremely nice memory filtered into her mind. "Speaking of that, I do remember waking up sometime during the night. You had your hand on my breast." And she hadn't bothered to remove it.

"I don't remember that, although it could account for the dream I had."

She'd had a few nice dreams of her own. "Was I in it?"

"What do you think?"

"I hope so." Yet she wanted to be more to him

than just the subject of his dreams. She wanted the reality.

"Take it from me, you were definitely there," he said.

"What were we doing?"

He patted her knee. "A guy's gotta have some secrets."

"Maybe we could have a reenactment tonight."

"Maybe you better get dressed so we can go fishing."

At least he hadn't said no, a positive sign as far as Jenna was concerned. After kicking the sheet away, she groped for her bag she'd left nearby and set it in her lap. "I need to wash up. Looks like it's back to the creek again."

"Not necessary," Logan said. "I hung a tarp between some trees a few feet away to give you some privacy. You'll find a pan of fresh water and a washcloth."

What a wonderful way to start the day—a spit bath. "Guess it will have to do, although I wish you would've packed an inflatable pool."

"The princess will have to manage."

She leaned over and pinched his thigh before rummaging through her bag. "You're asking for it, O'Brien."

"I'm kidding, Jenna. You don't have a spoiled bone in your body."

When she withdrew the travel-sized bottle of

shower gel, he snatched it from her grasp. "Aroma therapy?"

She held out her hand. "I'm willing to make some concessions, but not when it comes to personal hygiene. Now, give it back."

He placed the bottle in the well of her palm and curled her fingers around it. "Have a good time with your avocado and papaya scrub."

"Don't knock it unless you've tried it, Mr. O'Brien. It smells very good."

"Does it taste as good?"

"How should I know? I bathe with it, I don't drink it." She pulled a loofah from the duffel's side pocket. "And I wouldn't advise you taking a swig, either."

"I could always see how it tastes on your skin."

Jenna sensed his honor armor had begun to crack, and it wasn't even noon yet. "Is the 'friends only' thing getting old, already, Logan?"

He cleared his throat. "Not at all. I just momentarily forgot myself."

And. if Jenna had her way, he'd keep forgetting himself all day long.

Jenna stood on the creek bank wearing a pair of low-riding, high-on-the-thigh denim shorts, giving Logan a case of the can't-touch-that blues. Obviously she'd only packed one bra because she wasn't wearing one now, and that was almost too much for a man who'd been struggling to maintain his composure for the past sixteen hours. Not that he was counting the hours. Okay, he was.

If he made it through the day without putting his hands on her unless absolutely necessary, that would be just short of a miracle. But in order to show her how to cast, he'd have to touch her, just as he had with the camera the day before. So far she'd seemed content to chuck rocks in the water, something that would have to stop if they expected to catch anything. Teaching her how to fish in one morning could be challenging, but then they didn't have anything better to do.

In reality, they did, but he still wasn't ready to go there yet. Not until he'd proven he could control himself.

After baiting the line, Logan straightened from the tackle box and approached Jenna from behind. He hesitated a moment just to get a good view of her back and below. Damn, she had great legs and a great butt and if he didn't stop, he'd drop the damn fishing pole and his promise to go slow and steady. Slow and steady sounded about as appetizing as liverwurst for breakfast.

He came up close behind her, but not too close. "Are you ready to do some fishing?"

She glanced back at him. "I've been ready for at least fifteen minutes."

"I wanted to pick out the right lure," he said.

"It took a while. Now I'm going to show you how it's done."

"Oh, really?"

"Yeah, really." He placed the pole in her grasp and put his arms around her. Damn, she smelled good. "First of all, make sure you have a firm grip on the rod at all times, and keep it in the correct position."

She sent him a smile over one shoulder. "You know what they say. A well-positioned rod is hard to find."

He ignored the suggestive comment, even though his body had begun to take the bait. "I've already set the drag, so you won't have to worry about that. When you cast, the trick is to keep your motions smooth. You don't want to create a backlash."

"Let me see if I have this straight. You take the pole in hand, don't jerk it too hard and use a nice, fluid motion." She circled her fingers around the rod and stroked it. "I think I can manage that."

He started sweating like a marathon runner heading for the finishing line. "That's right."

"I do believe I have it."

So did he, and it was making him uncomfortable way down south. "Are you ready to try it?"

Again, she grinned. "Are we still talking about fishing?"

"You're killing me, Jenna."

"I don't mean to do that, at all, Logan." She reached back and patted his cheek. "But just so you know, if I hook a fish, I'm a firm believer in catch and release."

Logan had the catch down; now, if only he could release her. But the area at the back of her neck, exposed because she'd pulled her hair up into a ponytail, was just too damn appealing. Without thought, he lowered his head and kissed the spot, then worked his way around until he had her face in his grasp and his mouth on hers.

She discarded the rod and reel, turned easily into his arms and fitted herself so closely against him that he started calculating the distance to the nearest copse of trees. All the latent sexual energy he'd stored since last night came out in the kiss. All the arguments for avoiding this very thing jogged out of his head the minute she had her hands on his butt and he had his hands up her shirt to confirm she wasn't wearing a bra.

When he touched her breasts, she moaned against his mouth and pressed against his pelvis. His body's reaction was almost volatile and he went for the button on her fly, needing to know if she was as hot as he was. He had her zipper down in a flash and his hand was parting the placket, until a return of good sense—with a little help of voices from somewhere in the vicinity—forced him to reconsider.

He wasn't sure who was more winded, him or Jenna, when he stepped back and quickly readjusted her clothes.

Her disappointment was undeniable when she muttered, "And you thought Tahiti was crowded this time of year."

He had two choices—continue the fishing excursion, or take her back to the tent, away from prying eyes. He should go with fishing for two solid reasons, the first being that unless the condom fairy had left him a few underneath his pillow, he had no way to see this through completely. The second involved the friendship clause that he was in danger of severing if he didn't get his brain out of his jeans.

Jenna tightened her ponytail and picked up the rod, making the decision for him. "Maybe if we're lucky, the fish will still be biting."

Logan grabbed up his own rig and picked a place a few feet away from her. Without further instruction, she began casting like a pro.

"You're a quick study," he told her, in awe that even without her sight, she appeared to master anything she tackled.

"I've fished before, Logan," she said. "Several years ago, my dad and I took a couple of sport fishing trips to Mexico. I actually caught a Marlin once."

Anger set in. Anger that he couldn't quite explain. "You should've told me that before I went into instruction mode."

She continued to cast without missing a beat. "What, and miss all the fun of the post-instruction making out?"

"I'm serious, Jenna. You need to remember one important thing about me. I require total honesty."

She reeled in the line with a vengeance. "That's rich, Logan. You're asking me to be honest with you when you can't be honest with yourself."

"I don't know what you're talking about."

"Yes, you do, even if you can't own up to it."

She was still speaking in riddles. "Care to explain?"

After propping the rod against the rock that also housed her cane, she faced him. "You're hiding behind this whole friendship thing because the truth is, you're afraid of getting too close to a woman. And whether you admit it or not, Helena hurt you badly."

He didn't want to hear this. "She lied to me, Jenna. Sorry if that pisses me off."

She exhaled a slow breath. "I'm not her, Logan. I'm not going to fault you for your imperfections, because God knows I have plenty of my own. And I didn't come here to force you to do anything you don't want to do."

Without hesitation, and without any help from her cane, she walked toward him, stumbling slightly before she strode right up to him. "You might not understand this, but for years I've operated on the assumption that everyone knew what was best for me. Both David and my father treated me like a china doll incapable of functioning in the real world without complete dependency. I fought against it in the beginning, but I gave up to keep the peace."

She circled her arms around his waist. "But you're not like them. You've given me the chance to simply be me. To finally feel like a normal person and a desirable woman."

"You are a desirable woman, Jenna." And she didn't have a clue how much he wanted to fully uncover that side of her.

"That's why I'm going to keep reminding you that this chemistry between us is too powerful to ignore," she said. "My question is, when are you going to stop ignoring it?"

He rested his forehead against hers. "I don't want to hurt you in any way, Jenna."

"You don't want to be hurt again, and I don't want that, either. As long as we know going in that we're here to enjoy each other during the time we have left together, then neither of us will suffer for the decision." She smiled. "I don't want to leave here regretting that I didn't take full advantage of all the opportunities."

Logan found it uncanny how clearly she saw things. How clearly she saw through him, exposing facets of himself that he hadn't wanted to concede.

She'd been right on several counts, including the fact that the raw chemistry between them was too potent to disregard. And this time, he was going to prove that he could be both a lover and a friend. The friendship was already in place.

He kissed her quickly and said, "Pack up your things and let's get out of here."

Disappointment turned her smile into a frown. "You've decided to cut the weekend short."

His decision entailed giving her the best experience of her life. Maybe even his own life. "We're not going home, Jenna. We're going down the hill and we're going to find a cabin with a shower."

Her expression brightened. "Now, Logan, where's your sense of adventure?"

"You'll find that out when we're in bed."

Chapter Nine

After a four-hour trek back to the main campground, Jenna found herself sitting on the edge of a bed in a dark, musty and minimally cool cabin, alone. Logan had left with the directive for her to stay put until he returned in a few minutes. Although she wasn't certain of the time, or where he'd gone, she did know that more than a few minutes had passed. And she didn't want to wait to make good use of the shower.

She located the bag at her feet and withdrew essential toiletries, opting to forgo clothes. If Logan hadn't changed his mind, she wouldn't need them. She prayed he hadn't changed his mind. But if he didn't return soon, she might start believing that he'd left the state without her.

Jenna used her cane to guide her to the bathroom, not a difficult feat because the cabin—according to Logan—consisted of one area that housed the bedroom, a galley kitchen and a small living room.

Finding the walk-in shower wasn't difficult, either, considering it took up half of the tiny bathroom. She set her cane aside and felt along the wall to discover a towel draped on a rack mounted to the wall. Satisfied she had everything she needed, Jenna yanked back the narrow plastic curtain and felt for the metal handles. When she turned on the water, the scent of rust permeated the area and she hoped that her bath didn't result in orange-colored skin. But after she stripped and stepped under the spray, shampoo and shower gel in hand, the metallic smell disappeared and she only experienced the cool tile beneath her feet and blessedly warm, soothing water. Yet she only allowed herself a few minutes to relax before she soaped and shampooed away the grunge; she wanted to be waiting for Logan in bed when he finally came back to her.

After she rinsed and squeezed out her hair, she stepped onto the bath mat, reached for the towel and contacted only a barren metal bar.

"Are you looking for this?"

Jenna felt the slide of terry against her arm before she snatched the towel from Logan's grasp and began drying off—very slowly. "I didn't realize you were back."

"And I didn't realize you didn't understand my instructions." His voice sounded remarkably strained.

"I understood them." She wrapped up in the towel and tucked it between her breasts. "I just didn't see any reason to sit around and do nothing while you were gone. Which reminds me, where did you go?"

"I put the gear back in the Hummer, then I made a trip to the camp store."

"Did you get some things for dinner?"

"Yeah, and a few things for after dinner."

She suspected she knew the identity of those after-dinner "things." "I'm surprised they stock condoms at the camp store."

"They do, but they were out, which leads me to believe the Falstaffs are a wild bunch. I had to drive ten miles to the nearest convenience store."

At least that explained his lengthy absence. "Are you sure you didn't run into Liza Falstaff and have a quickie?"

"Not a chance. And since you didn't wait until we could shower together, it's my turn. I'm feeling pretty dirty right now."

Jenna admittedly felt a little dirty, too, and she was squeaky clean, at least physically. "If you want me to leave while you shower, I will. But if it's okay, I'd rather stay. I promise I won't peek." Oh, that she wished she could.

"You can stay and join me."

Not at all a terrible idea, but she wanted to build the anticipation for a bit longer. "Tell you what. Since the shower is barely big enough for one, much less two people, I'll stay and keep you company."

He tilted her chin up and kissed her gently. "There's plenty of room if you improvise. However, I wouldn't get much bathing done with you in there with me."

Jenna was highly encouraged by his comment. In a matter of minutes, she might finally experience what she'd wanted from him all along. "We'll save the improvising for later. In the meantime, I'll stand by while you wash away. Just leave the curtain open a little so we can talk."

"Not a problem, but I might get the floor wet."

"It's tile and I'm sure it's been wet before."

"Just stay right where you are so you don't slip and fall." He slid his fingertip down the cleft of her breasts. "You know, I can think of certain circumstances when wet is good."

Jenna backed up and reclined against the wall, needing its full support. "So can I. Now, hurry up."

"Yes, ma'am."

Since Logan appeared as an indistinguishable figure standing before her, she would have to rely on her imagination to form a cerebral portrait. She could also rely on him. "What are you doing right now?"

"Taking off my shirt."

She developed a mental picture compiled from her previous explorations of his chest, but she highly doubted it did justice to the real thing. When she heard the rasp of a zipper and the rustle of denim, she realized she didn't have a good frame of reference for how he might look at the moment. But she would soon, if she had any say in the matter.

After she heard the curtain sliding back, followed by the sound of water, she asked, "Are you washing?"

"Yeah, my hair."

"With my shampoo or yours?"

"Mine. Lavender smells a lot better on you than it does on me. And I have my own soap, too. A bar of soap, not gel."

She allowed him a few moments to finish that task before asking, "What are you doing now?"

"Bathing."

"I know that. What part of you are you bathing?" And that had to be the nosiest question she'd ever asked anyone.

"I'm scrubbing my face."

"Where will you go from there?"

":What do you mean?"

"Most people have a routine. For instance, face first, chest, legs and so on."

"I leave the 'so on' for last. Do you want to help me with that phase?"

She was assaulted by both heat and goose bumps simultaneously. "I trust you can handle that yourself."

"Much more fun if you'll handle it."

She resisted the urge to take him up on his offer. "I'll put that on my to do list."

"I'll remind you, just in case."

Closing her eyes, Jenna tipped her head back against the wall and let her fantasies take flight. She could picture him moving the soap over his body, across his broad chest, over his flat belly, down his solid thighs, then on to his perfect bottom. And after that... She wished she could be that bar of soap.

Jenna shifted her weight against the onslaught of damp heat and the rush of excitement. She had never wanted someone so much, specifically her former husband. During the early years together, their lovemaking had been satisfying for the most part, but never so hot that she'd felt as if she would crawl out of her skin if she didn't have him immediately. Right now, her skin was threatening to take a hiatus just thinking about Logan.

The desire he'd unearthed in her was almost frightening in its intensity. Perhaps that intensity resulted from the absence of intimacy in her life or the expectation of a memorable experience. Or maybe it was simply the man himself. A man who had taken time out of his busy schedule to escape with her for a few days, and she could only assume that the best of him was yet to come.

When the water stopped, Jenna's heart acceler-
ated and her respiration sounded strangely labored.
And when Logan touched her face, a low, needy
sound filtered out of her parted lips.

"Are you okay, Jenna?"

She inhaled deeply. "I don't know. I feel—"

"Aroused?"

"Yes."

He nuzzled his face in the bend of her neck.
"Tell me what you need."

His velvet-smooth voice was as effective as a
powerful potion, one that left her pleasurably weak.
"I need you take me to bed." Before her limbs no
longer held her up.

The words had barely left Jenna's mouth before
Logan gathered her into his arms and carried
her away in every sense of the word. He moved so
quickly, she had little time to prepare before he'd
deposited her onto the creaky bed. The mattress
bent beside her and following a tug, the towel fell
open, allowing a cool draft of air to flow over her
bare skin. When Logan rolled her onto her side and
into his arms, she absorbed the sensory details all
at once—the clean smell of him, the welcome feel
of him, the taste of him as his mouth covered hers.

His kiss was surprisingly restrained and brief
before he pulled back and grazed his lips along her
jaw, her neck and finally her ear. "I only have one
question to ask you before we go any further."

His tone was so somber, Jenna almost feared that question. "All right."

"What's your favorite color?"

She laughed from relief and utter joy. "Every color in the rainbow."

"I'll remember that," he said as he nudged her onto her back.

The conversation ceased with Logan's next kiss, a thorough yet incredibly gentle kiss. His fingertips skimmed her flesh, light and soothing as he raked them down her throat and over her collarbone. She almost issued a protest when he broke the kiss, but reconsidered when she experienced the warmth of his mouth closing over her breast. The soft workings of his tongue around her nipple urged a soft moan from her lips and his palm gliding down her belly prompted a slight shiver that ran the length of her body.

He turned his attention to her legs, brushing his knuckles back and forth on the tops of her thighs, coming closer and closer to the apex with each pass. She was on sensory overload, not quite knowing where to focus her concentration at the moment—on Logan's skilled mouth or his equally skilled hand.

Definitely his hand, she decided when he divided her thighs with his leg and centered his touch on the source of the ache that had plagued her for days.

"You're hot," he whispered.

She answered with a breathy, "Thanks to you."

"Tell me what else you want, Jenna."

"I want to touch you, too."

He lifted her hand and guided it to his erection. "Touch away."

And she did—with curiosity, with fine strokes as he did with her. She focused on Logan's reaction to her exploration and knew she was pleasing him simply by listening for the catch of his breath when she got a little bolder, yet worried she'd done something wrong when he tugged her hand away. "No more or I'm going to lose it," he said.

Jenna could very well say the same thing to him, if she had the presence of mind to speak, which she didn't since Logan hadn't halted his steady caress. The pressure began to build and build until she could do nothing more than surrender to the sensations. Yet Logan picked that exact moment to stop, eliciting a mild protest from Jenna.

"Not yet," he said.

She heard the sound of tearing paper, keenly aware that soon the wait would be over.

When he came back to her, Logan covered her body with his and said, "Now," as he lifted her hips and pushed inside her.

The climax hit her immediately with overwhelming authority, a release that completely consumed her and went on much longer than she'd expected. Only after the effects began to fade did she focus on the powerful thrust of Logan's body as she slid her hands down his back to his buttocks, delighting in the play of muscle against her palm. How much she'd missed this. How very, very much. More important, she was sorely reminded of her lack of vision and what that meant to their lovemaking.

"I wish I could see you," she said, and with all her heart, she did.

He stilled, raised her hands and kissed both palms before bringing them to his face, providing the means for her to observe his current state as best she could. "You feel so damn good," he said.

Even those few words seemed to cause him a great deal of effort, yet they moved Jenna more than she could express. And so did the heartfelt kiss he gave her immediately before he again gave in to his body's demands. As he drove deeper, harder, she continued to touch his face, wanting so badly to see the concentration in his expression, to witness the instant he was stripped of control. Instead, she relied on the rapid beat of his heart against her breasts and the tension in his frame that let her know the moment was close at hand. He climaxed with a hard thrust, shuddered and collapsed against her.

As Jenna rubbed his back and listened as his breathing slowed to a normal rhythm, she felt as if she had entered a place of peace that she never wanted to leave. A place where she could stay for a long, long time.

"What are you thinking?" she asked when Logan failed to move or speak.

"That was too rushed."

"That was pretty incredible."

"It could be better."

Any better and she might not have lived to tell the tale. "I don't agree, and it was definitely worth the wait." When he shifted slightly, she tightened her hold. "Don't go yet."

"I'm not going anywhere, and the wait is why it was too rushed."

She frowned. "We've known each other, for what, a whole seven days?" Oddly, she felt as if she'd known him much longer. "But then I suppose most women don't make you wait that long."

"Believe me, Jenna. You're nothing like most women."

The wooden headboard felt like a cement block against his back, but Logan didn't dare move or he risked ruining the moment.

After a light dinner consisting of cold sandwiches, he and Jenna had settled back into bed to talk. But somewhere along the way, while he'd been explaining to her about adding charter planes to his business plan, she'd fallen asleep, her head tucked in the crook of his arm, her hand resting loosely on his chest, her features slack. And that's where she'd been for over an hour, looking innocent and peaceful. For the past few minutes, he'd watched her eyes twitch behind closed lids and wondered what she was dreaming. If in those dreams she could see again.

He'd begun to realize she was a contradiction— fiercely independent and at times almost vulnerable, although, she tried to hide it behind her strong will. He could relate. No one wanted their weaknesses bared, especially not him. But he'd be damned if she hadn't chipped away some of his steel shell and made him care about something aside from business and temporary escapes in the beds of women he barely knew. She'd made him *feel* for the first time in a year—and that scared the hell out of him.

When Jenna turned away, Logan eased his arm from beneath her and carefully climbed out of bed. He slipped on a pair of shorts and walked to the refrigerator to find something to wet his dry mouth, craving a beer and settling for a bottle of soda—and some distance.

After sitting in the lone chair next to the aged plaid sofa, he set the drink aside, leaned his head back and closed his eyes. But he wasn't the least bit tired even though it was nearing midnight. In fact, he was too keyed up to sleep. And it was too bad the cabin didn't come equipped with a TV so he could find some ball game to occupy his mind. He could go for a walk, but he didn't want to leave Jenna alone. Or he could crawl back into bed, wake her up and expend some energy.

That thought alone brought his body back to life, but the sudden distressed cry brought his eyes wide-open to find Jenna sitting up in the bed, a frantic look on her face. He bolted from the chair and practically sprinted to the bed to hold her.

He rocked her back and forth until she seemed to calm. "It's okay, babe."

She pulled away, her expression a mask of confusion. "Logan?"

"Yeah, I'm here. You must've had a bad dream."

She streaked both her hands over her face, as if trying to erase the images. "It was a nightmare."

A really bad one, if the fear in her brown eyes was any indication. "Want to tell me about it?"

"It didn't make a lot of sense."

"Most dreams don't."

"I know, but this one was so strange and frightening." She inhaled a short breath and blew it out slowly. "I was in a small boat on the creek by myself and I saw J.D. on the bank. He looked exactly as he did the last time I could see him. I kept calling to him and when he saw me, he ran away into the woods. The next thing I knew I was chasing him and I couldn't find him. I had this horrible sense that something had happened to him and I couldn't protect him."

Logan realized that her subconscious was playing havoc with her fears. "Have you had this dream before?"

She shook her head. "Not exactly, but I've had a few that were similar. I'm hoping it's not some premonition, although I've never believed in that sort of thing before."

He kissed her forehead and held her tighter. "I'm sure he's fine. He's probably in bed asleep, which is where you and I need to be if we're going to get on the road early in the morning." With that thought, he reclined on the bed, taking her with him.

"I don't know if I can sleep until I'm certain John David's okay," she said. "And that won't happen until tomorrow night, if David even bothers to call me."

"Why wouldn't he?"

"Just to prove a point, which is typical of the Leedstone family."

Logan had to think a minute before he realized where he'd heard the name before. "As in Leedstone Electronics?"

"That's the one. He's in Memphis overseeing the opening of another phase of the dynasty."

Another instance of money marrying money. "Did you take your maiden name back after the divorce?"

"I never changed my name when we married. John David's last name is hyphenated."

Logan rubbed his chin. "John David Fordyce-Leedstone. Has a nice ring to it, but it'll never fit on a baseball jersey."

Finally, she smiled. A tentative one, but still a smile. "Anyway, David says I obsess too much over J.D. and that I tend to overreact. He's a fine one to talk considering how he treated me when we were married."

Alarm bells rang out in Logan's head. "Did he hurt you?"

"Only in the sense that I couldn't lift a finger without him questioning why I didn't ask for help, and that was when I could still see okay. He hired a nanny because he didn't trust I could take care of our child. But I did take care of him and I did it well."

The bastard. "I'm sure you did. My mother always said that maternal instinct is the strongest instinct in the world."

"Your mother is a very wise woman." She felt for his face and touched his lips with a fingertip, then with her own lips. "And she has a very special son."

He grinned. "Devin is a good guy."

She punched him in the arm, hard. "Stop pretending you're not worthy of a compliment, because you are."

Another one of his mother's lesson's intruded into his brain—accept praise graciously. "Thanks. You're kind of special, too." Kind of special? That was one hell of an understatement.

She linked her hand with his. "In some ways, I wish we didn't have to go tomorrow. But in others—and don't take this wrong—I'm looking forward to being home in time to talk with J.D."

Leaving the campground and leaving her, were the last things Logan wanted to consider at the moment. If it wasn't for the all-important communication with her son and Avery's insistence he bring her home tomorrow, he wouldn't mind extending the trip a few days. Then they could make the call to her son from his cell phone. He could ignore Avery's threats. Or they could…

Nah. That was a crazy plan. Insane. Impractical. But doable.

"Did you fall asleep on me, Logan?"

He rubbed her arm. "I'm still awake. I'm just thinking."

"About what?"

"About a phone call I need to make. The cell phone's on the charger in the car." He pushed out of the bed and tugged on his jeans. "I'll be back in a few minutes, so don't go anywhere."

She rolled to her side and played peekaboo with the sheet. "Maybe this will convince you to make it quick."

He leaned over and kissed her. "I'm convinced, and hold that thought."

She went one better and kicked the sheet entirely away. "A little added incentive."

The sight of her lying naked in a provocative pose made him hard as a steel beam. "You are one wicked woman."

"A lack of sight means a lack of inhibition, so get used to it, O'Brien."

Oh, yeah, he could definitely get used to it. He could also climb all over her, but first things first. "I'm leaving now," he said as he backed to the door. "Don't move."

"I promise I won't, if you'll hurry back."

He sprinted down the porch steps and hiked to the Hummer parked several yards away. He slid into the cab, detached the phone from the charger and hit the speed dial.

When Bob answered with a gruff, "Hello," Logan didn't bother to return the greeting. "I need you to do something for me, Bob."

"Where are you, boss?"

"Still in Arkansas. Go to your computer and look up David Leedstone's address and phone number in or around Memphis, Tennessee."

"That could take a while, boss, especially if the number's unlisted."

"Do what you have to do, but have it for me first thing in the morning."

"What's this all about?"

None of Bob's business. "Just get the address. And clear my schedule Monday. I probably won't be in until Tuesday morning."

"I see a big problem with that, Mr. O'Brien. You have a two o'clock meeting monday that we can't move again without losing a prospective client. You also have a meeting with Mr. Fordyce."

"I don't recall scheduling a meeting with him."

"You didn't. He did."

Great. "I'll be in on Monday afternoon, and I'll give Fordyce call."

And he would tomorrow, as soon as they were well on their way to Tennessee.

Chapter Ten

"How much longer before we're there, Logan?"

"My best guess is about five minutes."

Although the sun wasn't as bright as it had been when they'd left the park, Jenna sensed it wasn't all that late in the day. "What time is it now?"

"Almost six."

"I know we haven't been on the road for ten hours because we didn't leave until midmorning."

"Hey, our delayed departure wasn't my fault. You were the one who wanted to sleep in."

She felt an annoying blush coming on. "You didn't let me sleep."

"And I don't recall you complaining. Moaning, but not complaining."

She couldn't deny that, nor could she deny her continued confusion. "If my calculations are correct, we still have at least three hours to go before we reach Houston, not five minutes."

"I didn't say we were almost in Houston. I said we were almost there."

"Where exactly is *there?*"

"Hang on a minute. I need to concentrate." Logan braked and muttered, "Damn. I missed it," before he threw the Hummer in Reverse.

"Missed what?"

"The place we're going."

Jenna was growing increasingly frustrated with Logan's secrecy. "What place?"

"It's a surprise. You'll find out in a minute."

Occasionally, she liked surprises, but she had one vital issue on her mind. "If you're intent on stopping, I'll need to call J.D. from wherever we are."

"You're going to talk to your son tonight, Jenna. I promise."

All day long, she'd thought of little else aside from speaking with John David, when she wasn't thinking about Logan and what they'd shared over the past few days. Right now she wanted to give him a good tongue-lashing for being so mysterious.

When Logan took a sharp left, Jenna wondered if he'd found a notable restaurant. Maybe a hotel.

No, he'd said he'd planned to drive straight through. But straight through to where?

"We're here," Logan said, followed by the metallic clank of a releasing seat belt.

Jenna decided not to move until he provided some answers. "Could you please give me a little hint?"

"Okay. We're about to go inside a house and see some people about something."

She rolled her eyes. "That's not very specific, Logan. You should win an award for evasion."

He had the nerve to laugh. "Tell you what, if you're not happy with what I have planned, then you can tie me up later."

Somehow she didn't see that as adequate punishment. "You'd probably enjoy it."

"Could be. We'll discuss that later."

After Logan helped Jenna from the car, she heard the sound of dogs barking and children playing in the distance. She detected the scent of wisteria as they navigated what appeared to be a walkway.

"There's two steps up to the porch," Logan said.

After Jenna managed those without incident, she heard the chime of a doorbell—and an all too familiar voice saying, "It's good to see you, Jen," with little enthusiasm.

For a split second she'd thought her ears had betrayed her until Logan replied, "Thanks for having us on short notice, David."

"It's a little inconvenient, but come on in."

As they stepped over the threshold, Jenna's shock finally subsided and she regained her ability to speak. "What's going on?"

Logan caught her free hand and gave it a squeeze. "I promised you'd talk to your son, didn't I?"

Only then did Jenna allow herself to believe that Logan had granted her an incredible gift. She was going to be with John David, hold him, kiss him. She'd kiss Logan right now if her ex wasn't nearby.

"Where is he?" Jenna asked as she lowered her glasses from her head to cover her eyes against the harsh light in the foyer.

"He's in his room," a feminine voice answered. "Hi, Jenna. I'm Ginger."

Jenna found herself in the presence of the woman who'd entered J.D.'s life less than a year ago. A woman she'd never met nor seen before. The same woman who hadn't accompanied her new husband when he'd come to Texas to retrieve his son. "It's nice to finally meet you, Ginger."

"It's my pleasure," Ginger said as she took Jenna's hand for a brief shake. "But I'm afraid John David's rather tired from the trip right now. He's not in a very good mood."

Jenna knew how to remedy that. "Just point the way and I'll cheer him up."

"I'll see if he'll join us in the parlor," Ginger said.

"That's probably better, Jen," David chimed in. "He'll be more comfortable if we're with him."

If they were with him? For all intents and purposes, *they* were treating her like a stranger. "Fine, but I'd like a few minutes alone with him while I'm here."

"We'll see how it goes, Jen."

She wanted to tell David to quit shortening her name. At one time it hadn't bothered her, but now it grated on her already frayed nerves. "I'm sure he'll be fine once he sees me, David."

"I'll go get him," Ginger said. "In the meantime, make yourselves comfortable."

"A place to sit sounds good," Logan said. "It's been a long day."

"Right this way." David's tone reeked with forced politeness, and Jenna suspected he'd already begun to wonder about her relationship with Logan. As if that were any of his business.

Logan guided her to a sofa where she sat as stiff as a post and kept her opinions to herself. She couldn't let her anger get the best of her, not when she had the chance to be with her son.

Jenna's excitement increased when heard the endearing voice of the wonderful little boy she'd given birth to. The child she had loved, and still loved, without limits. And that precious son who'd always eagerly answered her phone calls suddenly cried out, "I don't know that lady!"

When she heard the rapid footsteps heading away, Jenna's heart began to break one fissure at a time. Her greatest fear had been realized—John David had forgotten her.

She couldn't bear knowing that her own child had rejected her when she'd come all this way to see him. She couldn't bear his distress, knowing she was causing it. Right then, she only wanted to get away.

As calmly as possible, she pushed off the sofa with the help of her cane. "This probably wasn't a good idea. Let's go, Logan."

Logan clasped her hand and tugged her back down on the couch. "Just give him a few minutes and let Ginger settle him down. Then you can go tell him a bedtime story."

"Jen's right, Logan," David said. "It isn't a good idea, and that's what I told you on the phone earlier."

"I don't give a damn what you told me." Logan's voice was even, but to Jenna it still sounded menacing. "She deserves some time with J.D., and once he understands it's really her, he'll be fine."

"I'm sorry, Jenna," Ginger said. "He refuses to come out of his room. Right now he's very upset. Maybe you should come back some other time."

Some other time. Ginger acted as though that were something Jenna could manage on any given day. "Thank you for making the effort, and tell John David I love him."

Again she stood and before Logan could stop her, she headed in what she hoped was the direction of the door, tapping her cane along the walls. The cloying scent of potpourri and polished wood caused her stomach to roil, along with the horrible notion that she'd lost the only thing that meant more to her than anything in the world, even her sight.

When she reached out and contacted the latch, a hand came out and stopped her before she could open the door. "Don't leave, Jenna. And don't listen to them."

Tears began to stream down her face despite her effort to hold them at bay. "He doesn't want to see me, Logan. He doesn't even know me."

Logan took her by the shoulders and turned her around. "He didn't get a good look at you. He'll only recognize you if you talk to him."

She swiped the back of her hand over her cheeks. "What if he doesn't?"

Logan brought her into his arms. "He'll remember you, Jenna. You only have to give him the chance to remember."

Jenna didn't know what to do. If she left now, she might regret it, or the same could apply if she stayed. But she had no idea when she would have this opportunity again.

"I'm sorry, Logan. You've gone to all this trouble for me, and the least I can do is make it worth your while."

"You need to make it worth your while, and it hasn't been any trouble at all. It might be if I lose my cool and punch your ex."

She clasped his hand and smiled. "You'd have to stand in line behind me. And if David does call the police, do you know a good bail bondsman in Tennessee?"

"He's not going to do that, and if he does, I'll take care of it."

For once Jenna didn't mind relying on someone for support. But Logan O'Brien wasn't just anyone, a fact that had become all too apparent in the past few days. "I guess, I could try."

"That's all you can do. And I'll be right there if you need me."

After they returned to the living room, David released a long-suffering sigh. "I thought the two of you had already left."

He was hoping they'd left, Jenna decided. "There's been a change in plans, David. Where's J.D.'s bedroom?"

"I thought we'd determined this was a bad idea."

Jenna was losing her tenuous hold on her patience. "I want to visit with my son tonight. If he sees me, he'll know it's me."

"I don't have to agree to this, Jen."

"You need to consider what's best for J.D.," Logan said. "And that's a visit with his mother."

"I am considering him, O'Brien, and right now he doesn't want to see either of you."

Jenna sensed movement in front of her right before Ginger said, "I understand how distressing this must be, Jenna, but I really don't think you want to upset John David further."

Jenna was on the verge of surrendering again until Logan asked, "How far along are you, Ginger?"

"Almost four months."

Setting aside her momentary astonishment and unreasonable bite of envy, Jenna decided to run with information Logan had provided. "How would you like it if someone kept you from your baby, Ginger?"

"I wouldn't."

"Then, let me have the chance to speak with my son. If he becomes too upset, I promise I'll leave."

"She's right, David," Ginger said. "She should have the opportunity to at least try."

"I don't like this one damn bit," David muttered.

Logan's grip tightened on Jenna's hand. "This isn't about you, Leedstone. Now, tell us where his bedroom is or I'll find it myself."

Jenna loved Logan for his concern. She loved that he'd given her this opportunity, no matter what the outcome might be. She loved…him? Now was not the time to examine that random thought.

"At the top of the stairs, second door to the left,"

David conceded. "But if he refuses, I want both of you back down here immediately."

Keeping her fury in check, Jenna gathered all the benevolence she could muster and said, "Thank you so much for *allowing* me to see my own child."

Logan took her by the hand and escorted her back through the corridor before he paused. "We're at the staircase. The steps are about two feet deep with about ten leading up the first landing and probably as many after that. Think you can make it on your own?"

Yes, she could, but she didn't care to. "Will you come with me?"

"If that's what you want."

"That's what I want." It's what she needed.

They ascended the stairs and traveled down a hallway before he paused and said, "We're at his bedroom. But let me go in first and talk to him."

"He doesn't know you, Logan." Jenna wasn't sure he would know her even after he got a good look at her.

"True, but I have a plan. Trust me on this, Jenna."

Somehow, she did. "Okay."

"I'll leave the door open so you can hear what I'm saying, but stay out of sight, for now."

When Logan left her, Jenna leaned a shoulder against the wall and listened.

"Hey, J.D."

"Who are you?"

He sounded wary and Jenna wanted to go to him now, hold him tightly, yet she held her impatience in check while Logan implemented his plan.

"My name is Logan, and I'm a friend of your mom's."

"Mommy Ginger?"

Jenna covered her mouth with her hand and squeezed her eyes shut against the tears.

"No. Your mom, Jenna."

"Oh. My *mama,*" he said, bolstering Jenna's confidence that he hadn't completely forgotten her.

"That's right. What's your bear's name?"

"Pookie Bear," Jenna mouthed at the same time as John David. The fluffy blue bear dressed in the sailor suit that she'd given him on his first birthday. The one he'd taken to bed every night since that time. At least that much hadn't changed.

"I used to have a brown bear that looked just like him," Logan said. "His name was Buzz."

Jenna couldn't imagine Logan with a stuffed animal. Tough guy Logan, the expert camper. The expert lover—and friend.

A span of silence passed before Logan asked, "Is this your mom in the picture?"

"Uh-huh. She's in Texas."

"She's right outside the door, buddy, and she wants to see you."

"She can't see me. Her eyes don't work."

She'd never kept that fact from him, but hearing

him say it, with such grown-up authority, stung something awful.

"But you can see your mom, bud, and she really wants to visit with you. Do you want me to go get her?"

"'Kay."

She heard approaching footsteps and felt Logan's touch on her arm. "He's sitting in the bed, which is against the far wall straight ahead when you enter the room. There's a chair on the left. The lamp's on the nightstand between the two, and I turned off the overhead light so you can take off your glasses."

Amazingly he'd thought of everything. "I appreciate that."

"I'm going to give you some time alone with him."

Jenna stood on tiptoe and kissed him lightly on the lips. "I owe you so much, Logan."

"You don't owe me anything. After all, that's what friends are for."

She smiled at the pride in his voice, although she realized she was dangerously close to wanting more than only his friendship. "Will you be right here?"

"I'll be back, but first I'm going to see if Ginger will make some coffee. We have a long night of driving ahead of us."

Jenna had assumed that maybe they'd find a place to spend the night and she could visit with J.D. tomorrow. But that was too much to ask. Logan had already taken a good deal of time away from his business to cater to her whims. "I'll see you in a bit, then."

"I'll be waiting. And take your time."

When she heard Logan sprint down the stairs, Jenna pulled off her sunglasses and pocketed them, smoothed a hand over her hair and drew in a fortifying breath. With cane in hand and a return of her courage, she walked into the room.

"How's my big boy?"

"Mama?"

"Yes, sweetie. It's me." She located the chair and perched on the edge. "I came a long, long way to see you tonight."

"Texas?"

She didn't feel the need to explain that she'd come by way of Arkansas. "That's right. Your dad told me you've grown a whole two inches this year."

"Uh-huh. I'm this big."

The bed creaked and she saw his hazy form not far away. "Can I have a hug?" She prayed for a yes and prepared for a no.

Her prayers were answered when John David crawled into her lap. And when his little arms came around her, she didn't want to let him go, although she did. Yet she was pleasantly surprised when he remained in the chair even after she released him.

She feathered his hair with her fingertips. "Did you have a good time on your vacation?"

He straightened and clapped his hands together. "I did!"

"Well, tell me all about it, then."

Jenna listened intently as he talked nonstop about the trip, the cartoon characters on board, the ocean and the beach. Through his childlike joy, she could imagine how wonderful the sights had been, how free he must have felt.

Following a lull in his enthusiastic recounting of the details, J.D. laid his head on her shoulder and yawned. He grew so still, Jenna assumed he'd fallen asleep in her arms, as he had so many nights not so long ago.

"Mama?"

Apparently she'd thought wrong. "Yes, sweetie?"

"Is my bed in Texas?"

"You have a nice bed in Texas, in a room with lots of toys at your Grandpa Avery's house. Do you remember him?"

"Nope."

She would have laughed over his cowboylike response, had she not been so distraught over how much he'd forgotten. "Anyway, it's a big house with a swimming pool. And someday soon, you can come to live with us again."

"When?"

"After I have my eyes fixed."

He traced a line below her lids. "You get new eyes?"

This time, she did laugh. "Only the parts that don't work."

He mulled that over for a time before he said, "Daddy told me I don't live in Texas anymore. I'm gonna go to school here and Mommy Ginger's going to give me a baby brother. But Daddy says you can come see me and my baby."

David had relegated her to visitor status, a phantom voice on the phone, a person who'd been in John David's life but wasn't any longer. Not in any real sense. And she would have something to say about that, but not now. Not when she had only a limited amount of time to enjoy these special moments.

Jenna swallowed around the tightening in her throat and gave him a squeeze. "How about I tell you a bedtime story?"

"'Kay. Then I go to sleep."

"Then you can go to sleep." She tucked away her sorrow and focused on the way he felt in her arms—so soft and warm and sweet. She would forget for a while that David and Ginger could give him things that she couldn't—a two-parent home, trips on big boats, a baby brother.

And as Jenna prepared to recite her son's favorite tale of wood sprites and fantastic creatures, she made a conscious effort to store this moment in her memory and house it with those she'd gathered throughout his young life. Because deep in her soul, she feared this could very well be the last time she would have the opportunity to hold her child.

"Where is my daughter, O'Brien?"

Thankfully Logan had stepped outside when the call had come in. "She's with me, and she's fine."

"Then why is she not answering her cell phone?"

Come to think of it, Logan hadn't seen her cell phone. "The battery could be dead." Or, she could be avoiding her father.

"How long before you arrive in Houston?"

"We still have a few hours to go because we're in Tennessee." Logan tipped the phone away from his ear in preparation for a minor explosion.

"What in the hell are you doing in Tennessee?"

Make that a major explosion. "I'm doing what you should have done a long time ago, letting her visit with your grandson."

"And why wasn't I notified of your change in plans?"

"I'm notifying you now. We'll be home in the morning. But you might want to reschedule our meeting in case I get stuck in traffic."

"The meeting is off, O'Brien. And so is the deal."

No real surprise to Logan. He'd known what he was risking when he'd chosen to take the detour on the way to Texas. "Not a problem, Avery. Jenna's more important than your financial backing."

"Exactly how important is she to you?" he asked suspiciously.

"She's my friend, Avery, and that's all." The words sounded false to Logan, in part because they weren't exactly true. "I have to go so we can get on the road."

"I don't like the thought of you driving all night."

"I've driven all hours of the night before without incident." Or they could get a hotel room, which would mean setting aside work for a little more pleasure and possibly losing more business in the process.

"I want my daughter home as soon as possible, Logan. And I'm holding you personally responsibile for her safety."

"I'll have her call you when we're in Houston."

Before he had to endure any more of Avery's reprimands, Logan flipped the phone closed and shoved it into the holder attached to his belt loop. The ten-hour drive was going to be tough, but after a few cups of coffee from the pot Ginger was making, he should be good to go. But he wasn't looking forward to tearing Jenna away from her child.

He also wasn't looking forward to confronting David Leedstone who'd suddenly appeared on the porch. He wore a go-to-hell expression as he leaned a shoulder against a column and shoved his hands into his pockets. "Tell me something, O'Brien.

How long has this thing with you and Jenna been going on?"

The man sounded a little too interested to Logan. "Jenna's a friend."

"Are you two sleeping together?"

"That's none of your damn business, Leedstone."

"That's what I thought."

Logan was tempted to wipe the smirk off the bastard's face. "Think what you will. Your opinion doesn't matter to me or to Jenna."

"I've seen the way you look at her, O'Brien. I know because I used to look at her that way, too. She's the kind of woman who gets under your skin. You want to protect her, but she won't let you. And if you get too close to her, she pushes you away because she automatically believes you're trying to run her life."

"I figure that's exactly what you did, Dave. Ran her life until you ran her off."

"It's David, not Dave. And did she tell you that?"

"She didn't have to, *Dave*. I saw a prime example of that tonight. You're a control freak and you hate the fact that she can survive without you. In fact, my guess is you're still in love with her."

David's face turned stone-cold. "You're wrong. I got over her the minute I met Ginger. And mark my words, if you're not in love with her now, you will be before it's all over."

Logan saw no reason to respond to the conjecture, even if it did bug him on some level. "I'm going to have some coffee, and then we're getting the hell out of here. I'd like to say it's been nice to meet you, but I'd be lying like a dog."

Before Logan could get through the door, David said, "I hope you are her friend, because she's going to need one in the next few weeks."

Logan turned around and glared. "What do you mean?"

"I'm putting you on notice that I'm filing for full custody of J.D. Jenna has no way of knowing when she'll receive the transplants, and our son needs to be in a stable environment."

Logan fisted his hands at his side, realizing he needed to leave now before the situation digressed any further. "Jenna needs to be with J.D., and I'll see you in hell before I let you take that from her."

Before Logan made it through the door, David called him back. "You're right about one thing, O'Brien. I did love Jenna at one time, and a part of me always will love her because she gave me J.D. And I'm not as unreasonable as you might think. I'm not doing this to hurt her. I only want what's best for my son."

Leedstone's admission only added fuel to the fire burning in Logan's gut. "If you cared about her, at all, then you wouldn't even consider keeping J.D. away from her."

Without waiting for a response, Logan tore into

the house and up the stairs at breakneck speed. He paused outside the bedroom and harnessed his anger before opening the door.

The scene playing out before him only cemented Logan's concern for Jenna. With her eyes closed and J.D. asleep in her arms, she looked serene, totally unaware of what the future might hold. And the worst part was, she had no clue that, if David Leedstone had his way, this could be the last time she'd hold her child until the custody war had been won—or lost.

No matter what he'd said to Leedstone a few minutes before, this wasn't his fight, and he couldn't do a damn thing about it. Not unless Jenna invited him into the battle.

Chapter Eleven

Jenna had slept on and off most of the journey, and when she'd been awake, she'd been unusually quiet. But then, so had Logan.

For ten hours straight, his mind had reeled with the knowledge he held, and whether to share it with Jenna. He felt certain she was still oblivious to Leedstone's plans. Nothing had been said aside from forced goodbyes when they'd left. And now Logan was charged with telling her the sorry news, as hard as that would be on her. No one knew bitter betrayal better than him.

When they reached the city limits, the stop-and-go Monday-morning traffic bought Logan a little more time before he dropped her off at the estate and provided the opportunity to make the revelation he didn't want to make. But she deserved the truth.

He glanced at Jenna to find she'd put on her shades to protect against the rising sun. But he could tell she was awake from the way she thrummed her nails on the console.

He reached over and clasped her hand not only to still her movements, but also to provide some support. "Your ex-husband's an ass."

She smiled. "He's not really that bad most of the time. In fact, he used to be very charming. I'm not sure why he acted the way he did last night."

"He has a guilty conscience."

"Why would you say that?"

Damn, he hated doing this to her, but he didn't have a choice. "He told me he's going to file for full custody of J.D." He expected an angry response, maybe even tears, yet she only continued to stare out the windshield. "Did you hear what I said?"

"My ears are working fine. I'm just not surprised. John David basically told me the same thing."

No wonder she'd been so sullen on the drive. "He told you about the custody issue?"

She released a humorless laugh. "He's smart, Logan, and very articulate for a three-and-a-half-year-old. But he's not quite that smart. David told him he lived in Tennessee now, not Texas, and that

I could visit. He also said in so many words that he doesn't want to live with me."

Damn Leedstone to hell. "And that doesn't bother you?"

"Of course it bothers me. It tore my heart out. But David might be right."

Logan hadn't anticipated the defeat in her tone, and hearing it made him sick inside. "He's wrong, Jenna. J.D. belongs with you."

"I'm not sure he does. Visual impairment and a child is a terrible combination, which is probably why my biological mother gave me up for adoption."

"You don't know that your mother was blind."

"No, I don't know for certain. But my instincts tell me she was and she made the decision based on what she thought was best for me."

"I'm not going to let you give up, Jenna."

She swept her hair back with one hand. "It's not your decision to make, Logan. And honestly, I'm too tired to discuss it."

He decided to let it go, for now. "You'll be home in fifteen minutes, then you can sleep the rest of the day."

"I'd rather go to your place."

Logan could foresee one major problem with that. "Your dad's already royally pissed off. If he learns that you—"

"I'll call him, unless you don't want me to come home with you."

If he said he didn't, he'd be lying to her and to himself. "My condo it is."

Jenna rifled through the bag at her feet, withdrew her cell phone and spoke the simple word *home*.

"Hi, Dad. We're in Houston, but I won't be there for a while. I'm going to cook breakfast for Logan at his place and I'll let you know when I'm heading home. Bye." She slapped the phone closed and dropped it into the bag.

"It didn't sound like you gave him a chance to say anything."

She shrugged. "I didn't. And since I can't make toast without cremating it, I seriously doubt he bought the breakfast thing. But I certainly couldn't tell him the truth."

"What is the truth, Jenna?"

She leaned over and laid her hand on his thigh. "The truth is I don't want to be in my bed. I want to be in yours until it's time for me to go."

Logan got the feeling she could be on the verge of ending their involvement before the day was done, right when he was contemplating the possibilities. He'd just have to work hard to prevent that from happening, and he had several ways to do that. For the next few hours, he planned to try every one.

When they pulled into the parking garage a few minutes later, Logan left most of the gear in the SUV while Jenna slung her smaller bag over her shoulder, leaving her cane behind. They entered the elevator with a group of people and stood side by side in silence until the only remaining couple exited on the fourth floor. As soon as the doors slid shut, Logan couldn't stand it any longer. He kissed her all the way to the ninth floor and only let her go long enough to unlock and open the door. And when they stepped inside, he kissed her some more.

In the interest of saving time, Logan lifted Jenna into his arms and carried her up the stairs—stairs that he always took two at a time, a routine act he'd taken for granted. Since he'd met Jenna, he'd begun to recognize all the challenges she faced on a daily basis, and that had only reinforced his appreciation of her.

He definitely appreciated her sexy smile after he set her down on her feet in his bedroom. "Where's the shower?" she asked.

"Right behind you." Logan pushed her hair back and kissed her neck. "We're going to take one together this time."

"Definitely."

After he backed her into the bathroom, they undressed as if competing in a race to see who could finish first and, remarkably, Jenna won, while Logan balanced on losing control.

Even in light of his exhaustion, he honestly believed he could drop to the ceramic-tiled floor and do a hundred push-ups—or take her on the floor right where they stood. He chalked that up to pure adrenaline. To Jenna.

With what strength he had left, he led her into the shower where he opted for limited foreplay. Just enough to taunt her while they bathed, before he pulled out all the stops. But she wasn't making it easy when she did some pretty creative things with her hands. In fact, she was making it extremely hard. And he returned the favor until he had her digging her nails into his back.

"The bedroom," he told her before things got too out of hand.

"Good idea," she said, and gave him a quick pinch on his bare butt.

They barely dried off, didn't bother with clothes and hit the bed without turning down the covers. As they faced each other, no words passed between them and it wasn't because they had a hard time talking to each other; they'd had several good conversations over the course of the weekend. Logan had plenty to say to her, just not now.

He didn't need words. He needed to hear the sound of her sighs when he touched her and the rapid rhythm of her breathing when he kissed his way from her neck to her breasts and then down her belly. Using his mouth, he brought her to the brink, then let up until he knew she couldn't take any more. He had her precisely where he wanted her—completely under his influence and in a place she wouldn't soon forget. Or so he thought until she nudged him onto his back and levied a little persuasion of her own.

He gritted his teeth and hissed out a breath when she did to him what he'd done to her. She didn't hold anything back, didn't miss an inch of his skin with her deadly kisses, and by the time she shimmied up his body, he was ready to wave a white flag.

He rolled away from her to retrieve a condom from his nightstand and after he tore open the packet, she held out her hand and said, "Let me."

Yeah, she was definitely the one in command, and that became even more obvious as she straddled his body, taking him inside her.

She began to move, and Logan detected a hint of desperation. But then he felt a little desperate, too. Desperate to understand why she affected him in ways no woman ever had.

He couldn't consider that now. He couldn't consider anything except Jenna hovering above him, her hair hanging down in damp strands around her face, her lips slightly parted, her eyes closed tight. She drove him to the edge with the rise and fall of her hips. Her smile indicated she knew exactly what she was doing and where she planned to take them both. Her lack of inhibition, her determination, her periodic kisses, hurled them to that destination quickly. The pulse of her climax brought on his own, a force that ripped through Logan and drove every lucid thought from his brain.

As Jenna buckled against him, his arms came around her, and as he continued to hold her, he couldn't shake the guilt over what he'd done the past twelve months. Although he'd been discriminating when it had come to his lovers, he'd also been a jerk, no better than his youngest brother who'd made sex a sport. And among the half-dozen women Logan had taken to bed, he'd never been sorry to see one of them go.

But today, as he started to drift off to sleep with Jenna's body curled into his, he never wanted her to leave.

Jenna awoke with a start when she heard an annoying buzz. She shook Logan's arm and whispered his name, yet he didn't respond. She wasn't all that surprised. He'd been on the road all night and his exhaustion had finally gotten the best of him. Their lovemaking had also been a contributing factor. Even so, if she had her way, she'd ask him to do it all again, at least one more time before she left for good.

The buzzer sounded again, sending Jenna from the bed to follow the noise originating from the hall outside the bedroom. She felt along the wall until she located the intercom. After depressing the button, she said, "Yes?"

"Miss Fordyce?"

The man sounded as surprised to hear her as she was to hear her name. "That's me."

"Uh, there's a man down here named Calvin. He says he's supposed to take you home."

Clearly, her father had called out the guard. "Tell him I'll be down in about five minutes."

And that was just as well. This little bit of paradise with Logan was almost over. It had to be. She had too much going on in her life and not enough confidence to believe that she could be the woman he needed—even if she'd tried to fool herself into thinking that was possible. He deserved a woman who was whole, both physically and emotionally.

After she located her bag and dressed in the last of her clean clothes, a blanket of depression settled over her. Tonight, she would again go to bed alone and wake tomorrow alone. But the decision weighing heavily on her mind was one she had to make by herself. The most difficult decision she would ever have to make—relinquishing custody of her child.

After one more futile attempt to wake Logan, she left the room and carefully descended the stairs. She relied on her learned ability to mentally chart a course of places she had been before, the steps she had taken, in order to find the front door. As she waited for the elevator, she chastised herself for leaving Logan without any explanation. But she couldn't very well write him a note; her handwriting was barely legible these days. And knowing him, which she did—better than she ever dreamed she would know him—he would call her later and demand an explanation. Yet she wasn't certain she could explain her feelings to him because she didn't know how she felt, aside from confused. She did know that in the limited time she'd spent with him, she'd never been so happy. So liberated. So close to falling in love.

"Were you going to leave without saying good-bye?"

Jenna turned to the sound of his voice, as if he had some magnetic hold over her. "I didn't want to wake you up." She didn't want to say goodbye, either. "Dad sent Calvin for me. He's waiting downstairs."

"I can drive you home on the way to my office."

She shook her head. "That's not necessary, Logan."

"Fine. I'll call you later."

"That's not necessary, either."

"I know that, but I want to."

When he circled his arms around her waist, she wanted to ask him not to touch, otherwise she would never be able to do what she had to do. Yet she couldn't force herself to pull away from him.

"We can go out to dinner tomorrow night. Or I can take you to the baseball game. I have good seats. I'll nab a fly ball for you as a souvenir."

He simply didn't get it, and that couldn't be more

apparent to Jenna at the moment. "I couldn't see a fly ball coming at me, Logan. I couldn't even see any of the action."

"I'll give you a play-by-play."

Gathering her strength, she wrested out of his grasp. "We've had a great few days together, but now it's back to the real world. And my reality isn't very pretty."

"What the hell are you saying?"

"You were absolutely right. Lovemaking complicates everything. It's better we end it now before someone starts caring too much."

"It's too damn late for that, Jenna. You've already made me care, like it or not."

She prayed the elevator would hurry and arrive, before she completely broke down. "I'm a mess, Logan. My life's a mess. I may lose my child. I may never regain my sight."

"You don't have to go through this alone. I'm willing to be there for you."

He'd proved that to her yesterday, but still… "It's my problem, Logan. You don't need the hassle."

"Don't presume to tell me what I need. But I'm going to tell you something and you need to listen carefully." His tone reflected anger yet contrasted with the gentle way he touched her face. "After Helena and I broke it off, I spent a year trying to convince myself that I could survive by moving from one woman to the next. But it didn't do anything to cure my loneliness. In fact, it made it worse. And then I met this sexy, determined, hardheaded beautiful woman and I didn't feel alone, anymore."

She closed her eyes and willed away the tears, at least for the time being. "Please stop, Logan. You're only making this more difficult."

"This whole thing's difficult, Jenna, and I didn't plan on it happening. But whether you meant to or not, you made me feel something for the first time in a long time and I'm not willing to blow that off."

The elevator chimed, providing her with the out she so desperately needed. "I'm sorry, Logan," she said as she backed up a step, "I can't do this. I don't know what else to say."

"You don't have to say anything else. I get it now. We had a great time, it was a nice diversion, and that's it. At least for you."

If he only knew how wrong he was. "It wasn't only a diversion, Logan. It was—"

"Don't try to come up with something to make me feel better, because I'm still going to feel like hell. Have a nice life, princess. And good luck."

Jenna entered the elevator not knowing if Logan was still there, or if he'd already left. Her eyes were so clouded with tears that she couldn't detect the boldest movement or the darkest shadow. She felt along the bank of buttons and, using her Braille, found the one that indicated the lobby.

She had learned to manage her life as best she could. She had worked hard to maintain some normalcy as an unsighted woman in a visual world. Yet she couldn't help but wonder if by walking away from Logan, she was blind to what could be the best thing that had happened to her in years.

He found her tending to her garden, as he knew he would. Lucine Kabakian O'Brien always spent every morning from March through August pruning her plants with the same commitment she'd shown to her family.

From a very early age, the O'Brien boys had learned to seek out their father for guidance on sex and their mother for counsel on affairs of the heart. Logan needed that counsel now more than any time in his adult life.

She kept her back to him, still totally unaware he'd entered the yard. And when he walked toward her, bent down and popped a kiss on her cheek, she spun around and gasped.

"Heavens, Logan. Don't you know better than to startle a woman with pruning shears? That's a good way to lose all hope of fathering children."

He slid his hands into his pockets and sent her a sheepish smile. "Sorry, Mom. I didn't mean to scare you."

"You're forgiven, dear." She tossed the tool into the nearby cart and worked the gardening gloves from her hand. "Your father is always sneaking up on me. I thought you were him."

"He told me to tell you he's reading the morning paper."

She sent him a skeptical look. "He's in the lounger, taking his morning nap."

Logan grinned. "Yeah, he is. And before I left the living room, he started snoring as loud as a turbo-charged engine."

"Nothing new there." She gestured toward the patio with a glove. "While he's occupied, let's have a nice chat. Just the two of us."

She hooked her arm through his and after they were seated in two chairs opposite each other at the small table, Logan leaned forward and clasped his hands together on the metal surface. "I wanted to apologize for not being here the past two Sundays for lunch and for not calling."

She studied him with concern. "It's more than that, Logan. Something is terribly wrong."

He wasn't surprised by her ability to read him. She'd owned that talent for as long as he could remember. "I'm having a tough time right now." Tougher than he'd expected since he'd said good-bye to Jenna. He'd been doing a good impression of a lovesick idiot and he didn't know why. Maybe it was only wounded pride. After all, he was usually the one to call things off with a woman, not the other way around.

"I distinctly remember the last time you surprised me with a morning visit," Lucy said, breaking into his thoughts. "You told me you were planning to marry Helena and you wanted suggestions on how to propose."

That was a sorry subject he'd rather avoid. "And it turned out to be a huge mistake."

Lucy laid her palm on his arm, garnering his attention. "This little visit doesn't involve another woman, does it? Perhaps a pretty, down-to-earth young woman whom we met and fell in love with two weeks ago?"

Jenna had predictably received the O'Brien family stamp of approval. "Yeah, it does."

He launched into a summary of the camping trip, the visit to Tennessee and ended with Jenna's insistence she didn't need anyone to support her through the custody battle. "Anyway, I haven't talked to her since."

"You haven't even tried to call her?" His mother sounded astounded and a little disappointed.

Truth was, he'd picked up the phone every day for almost two weeks, sometimes two or three times a day, and he'd hung up before the first ring every time. "I don't want to push her."

"There's a difference between pushing, Logan, and letting her know you care. And I suspect you care much more than you're willing to admit."

She'd hit that nail straight on the head. He afforded her a quick glance before lowering his gaze to the table, something he hadn't done since his early teens, when he'd awaited punishment for toilet papering the principal's front lawn. "When did you know you wanted to spend the rest of your life with Dad?"

"You're asking me to think back to a time when George Washington was still wearing knickers?"

Logan laughed over her use of one of his father's favorite phrases. "I guess, I assumed that was something you wouldn't forget."

She smiled. "No, I've never forgotten. I was a very shy girl in school and I didn't know any boys at all. Then out of the blue, your father asked me to the senior dance. Funny thing was, he didn't even know how to dance, but that didn't stop him from trying. I suffered a few sore toes that night, but I also fell in love with him. A tough, loud Irishman who was willing to risk embarrassing himself in order to make me happy. We married three months later, I became pregnant with Devin three months after that, and he's been making me happy ever since."

That was a story Logan had never heard, but he'd never thought to ask before he'd met Jenna. "Only three months before you two married?"

"Yes, and I would have married him the day after the dance if he'd asked me." Her expression turned serious. "Love doesn't stop to consider how long you've known a person, Logan. Sometimes it never arrives. Sometimes it doesn't come about for years. Other times it hits you immediately. And that was much the case with me and your father. Is that what's happened with you and Jenna?"

Logan still had a hard time wrapping his mind around that concept. "I don't know, Mom."

"Tell me something. Are you finding you can't sleep? Do the things you like to do no longer give you joy? Are you having trouble concentrating at work?"

She had a surplus of insight for such a small woman. "All of the above."

"Did you find yourself watching her while she was sleeping?"

"I never said I slept with her."

It was his mother's turn to laugh. "My dear child, all my sons are genetically predisposed to uncontrollable passion when it comes to women, thanks to your father."

He damn sure didn't want to get into this. "It's not about sex, Mom. It's more." Okay, he'd said it, and the house behind him didn't cave in.

"Then, you are most likely in love with her."

"I didn't intend to be anything but her friend."

Lucy clasped his joined hands. "Be her friend, honey. Give her a little more time, but not too much time, then pay her a visit and let her know you want to be there for her. What's the worst that could happen?"

He knew the answer to that. She'd tell him to get the hell out of her life.

But as it had been with building a successful business, nothing worth having had ever come easily. And Jenna was worth one more try.

He'd give her some time, and then he was going to give her something he'd never given to another woman, not even Helena—his heart.

Chapter Twelve

"I'm worried about you, sweetheart."

The same song and dance from her father she'd endured myriad times over the past two weeks. "I'm going to be all right, Dad. You don't have to worry."

"You're not all right, Jenna. You barely eat. You haven't been out in days."

"I went to the eye doctor on Thursday."

"But you didn't go to the library to tell the children stories. And I want to know right now what Logan O'Brien did to you to cause you this much distress."

She leaned her head back in the chair and groaned. "My current state of mind doesn't have anything to do with Logan." And that wasn't completely true. She'd had no idea she could miss someone so much—someone she'd known such a brief time.

"You were fine before you went on that trip. If you hadn't gone—"

"Then I would have been surprised when the custody documents showed up on the doorstep. At least I was prepared." Or as prepared as she could have been in light of the situation.

"But you haven't signed them yet."

She pinched the bridge of her nose between her thumb and forefinger. "No, I haven't signed them." Giving up the right to raise a child was no small task. She had to be certain she was willing to go that far in order to ensure her son's well-being, although the way things stood, she didn't feel she had an alternative. David had more to offer, and J.D. preferred David over her.

"You need to focus on the good news. We've waited so long for you to move to the top of the donor list."

And that was something else she'd thought about incessantly. Another decision that had weighed her down. "I'm considering being removed from the list."

"You can't be serious."

The alarm in her father's voice came as no surprise. "Yes, I am."

"But if you don't go through with the surgery, you have little chance to retain custody of J.D."

"I don't feel I have much of a chance now." She didn't feel as if she had any hope left. "Besides, being at the top of the list doesn't guarantee I'll have the transplant immediately. It could be years from now."

"It could be tomorrow."

"I realize that, but it's not likely. And the thought that, someday, someone will suffer a tragic accident or irreversible brain damage so I can see again, isn't pleasant."

"I don't understand your attitude, Jenna. You've always been a fighter, and now you're giving up."

She could understand why he would view it that way. She wasn't giving up; she was simply resigned to her future. A future without sight, without more children. She could still have a good life. She could still visit J.D. twice a year, maybe more. But would that ever be enough to maintain a relationship with him? "I'm tired, Dad. I want to go to my room and finish an audio book I've been listening to."

"More Italian lessons?"

She hadn't seen any need for more of those lessons. The European trip seemed as improbable as having J.D. living with her again. "It's a true-crime novel."

"Are you going to call John David?"

Oh, how she longed to do that very thing. "No, Dad, I'm not. If he wants to speak with me, he'll call."

"He's three and a half years old, Jenna. He doesn't know how to make a long-distance call."

How well Jenna knew that. But when she'd attempted to call the past few nights, all she'd received was voice mail. David had already set the wheels in motion to effectively drive her child out of her life.

Too weary for anger or more revelations, Jenna slid her chair away from the table and hoisted herself up with the cane. "Have a nice night, Dad."

"I knew when I allowed you to go on that trip with Logan, something like this would happen. I knew he would get what he wanted from you and then toss you aside. He doesn't realize how special you are and he's beaten you down. That's why you're so depressed."

Suddenly she wasn't so tired that she couldn't get mad. "You don't know what you're talking about, Dad. Logan was absolutely wonderful during our trip. He gave me space and let me be me the whole time. He knew how much I missed John David and he took me to see him. He's done nothing wrong."

"Except for breaking off all ties with you."

She tightened her grip on the cane. "He didn't break it off. I did. He's a good man, Dad. He's a great man. And he doesn't deserve to get caught up in my chaotic life."

When her father failed to respond, for a moment she'd thought he'd left the room and she wished he had when he said, "You're in love with him."

Unfortunately, that was true. "It doesn't matter how I feel about him. It's over between us, and there's no going back."

If she had the opportunity, she might take it all back. If she'd known how it was going to turn out, she might have never said yes to the lunch at his parents, the walk in the garden. The camping trip.

But that wasn't accurate. Regardless that their relationship had been severed, and with good reason, she'd never take back one moment of their time together. And she'd never stop wondering what might have been.

Logan had waited long enough to tell her how he felt about her, but that was about to end. After grabbing the receiver, he pounded out the number he'd dialed numerous times—only, today, he wasn't about to hang up.

"Fordyce residence."

Logan recognized the woman's Eastern European accent from the last time he'd called. "I need to speak to Jenna." His mother's lesson on the importance of manners came into play. "Please."

"May I ask who is calling?"

He considered withholding that information, then decided honesty was the best policy in this case. Even if it meant Jenna refusing to talk to him. If that happened, he'd keep calling until she finally caved. "Logan O'Brien."

"One moment, please."

He waited for what seemed like an eternity before someone finally answered—and that someone wasn't Jenna.

"My daughter doesn't want to speak with you, O'Brien."

Apparently, Avery didn't, either. Fordyce hadn't contacted him since their conversation in Tennessee. Fortunately, he hadn't severed the business ties, either. Not yet, anyway. "Did you ask her if she'd take my call?"

"I don't have to ask her. She told me last night that the two of you are finished with whatever was going on between you. But, while I have you on the phone, I have something I have to ask you."

Logan had expected as much. He'd let Avery have his say, hang up and try Jenna's cell phone. "Fire away."

"What in God's name did you say to her to convince her she didn't need the corneal transplants?"

That he hadn't seen coming. "I don't know what in the hell you're talking about, Avery."

"At her doctor's appointment this afternoon, she claims she's going to request to be taken off the list.

And don't try to tell me you had nothing to do with that decision."

"Believe me, Avery. That's the last thing I would tell her to do."

"Well, someone wielded some influence. I can't believe, after all the waiting, she would decide on her own to halt the process."

Logan couldn't believe it, either, or he wouldn't have two weeks ago. But he had a theory on what had changed her mind. "Did she mention her ex-husband's plan to get full custody of J.D.?"

"Of course she did. The documents came two days ago. If she signs them, it's a done deal. If she doesn't, she'll face a court battle. And if she refuses to correct her vision, she might not win."

One other key to Jenna's attitude switch had yet to be broached, and now was a good time for him to bring it up. "If anyone's partially at fault for Jenna changing her mind, it's you, Avery."

"You have a lot of nerve saying that to me."

He had a lot of nerve making accusations about Jenna and him that he couldn't prove. "Whether you mean to be a contributing factor or not, you are through your refusal to tell her about her biological mother."

"I don't see how that's relevant or any of your business."

Logan tightened his grip on the phone and silently rehearsed several oaths. "Jenna has it in her head that her mother gave her up because she had the same disease. She firmly believes that the unselfish thing to do would be to give up J.D. for the same reasons. On some level, I get why she might feel that way, but only if she had no chance to regain her sight."

Avery sighed. "The transplants carry a risk of rejection and the disease could return in a matter of years, even if the surgery is successful. She could require another transplant if that happens."

At least some of this was beginning to make sense. "I also suspect she has some heavy-duty guilt over possibly passing the disease on to J.D."

"According to the eye specialists, we have no way of knowing unless we have an extensive family history."

"And that brings me back to my point. You've got the money and the means to track down Jenna's mother. Why haven't you attempted it?"

"I did several years ago, only to learn she died long before Jenna started having trouble with her vision."

"Then you know who she is."

"According to the agency, she was a strung out runaway who lived on the streets of Atlanta. She had no idea who Jenna's father was and, to this day, that remains a mystery. But I also know she wasn't blind. She was a lost cause, and that led to her death two years after Jenna was born."

Avery's motivation behind concealing the information was much more evident to Logan, and understandable, even if he didn't agree with his reasoning. "You were trying to protect her."

"Yes, I was, and I realize now that was probably a mistake."

"You could rectify that mistake by telling her the facts, before it's too late to matter."

"I'm not sure she can handle more bad news."

Logan would have argued that point the day he met her, but not now. "You can at least assure her that her mother wasn't blind without getting into all the ugly stuff."

"I might have a solution to everything. When we brought Jenna home, the agency sent a letter from her mother with her. It's not pretty, but it does explain why she chose to put Jenna up for adoption and that she'd wanted to keep her, but couldn't."

Unbelievable. "She's never read it?"

"No. I almost gave it to her several times, but I couldn't bring myself to do it. I didn't want to hurt her."

Logan wanted to yell at Avery for not seeing what his daughter needed. "You might hurt her more in the long run if you don't tell her the truth now."

"I know. And you might not understand this, Logan, but everything I've done for Jenna, I've done because I love her, wise or not."

Logan understood it more than Avery realized.

In fact, what he planned to do was a direct result of his love for her—a love he'd tried to deny until his mother's wisdom had forced him to own up to it. "Where is Jenna now?"

"The place she goes every time she wants to think. Her mother's garden."

With the sun on the rise in the midmorning sky, she knew she should go back inside before the rays became intolerable. Yet Jenna continued to sit on the wrought iron bench, immersed in the fragrance of roses and memories of the woman she'd called "Mama." A woman who may not have given her life, but had provided her with an abundance of love.

Jenna recalled the times she would come to the garden with her mother to play hide-and-seek, a tradition she'd continued with John David not long after he'd learned to walk, while she'd still been able to watch him. Now, more than ever, she longed for her mother's shoulder to cry on to help alleviate the unshakable loneliness and confusion. Her father was trying, she'd give him that, but it simply wasn't the same. Although his heart was in the right place, he didn't understand he couldn't protect her from everything and that only she could decide what was best for all involved.

The echo of footsteps brought Jenna's musings to a standstill. Heavy footsteps that led her to be-

lieve the approaching party was male with an un-
known identity. Her father had surely left for work
and the yard crew never came on Tuesdays. Still,
Jenna doubted some dangerous intruder had infil-
trated the high-tech security system surrounding
the estate. "Who's there?"

"Logan."

Even if he hadn't identified himself by name, she
would have begun to sense him as he moved closer.

"Mind if I sit down."

Jenna probably should mind, but she didn't.
She probably should ask him to leave, but she
couldn't. "Be my guest. You can tell me why
you're here."

He settled in beside her, an obscure image in her
ever-failing field of vision. Yet his presence was
somehow comforting. "I need to talk to you about
something."

"You could have called." In spite of what she'd
told him when they'd parted, she'd longed for that
call, that last little attempt to win her over.

"It's hard to reach someone by phone when you
have a father running interference."

"You called me?"

"This morning. Turns out that after your dad insisted you didn't have anything to say to me, we
had a long conversation, at which time he informed me you're not going through with the
transplants."

Now she understood. He was here because her father had recruited him. "I see. The resident white knight has come to talk me into having a surgery I'm not sure I want to have. There are worse things than being blind, Logan."

"I agree, particularly if you can't see the good because you're too focused on the bad."

"I only see my life as this series of decisions I can't seem to make."

"Then you're not altogether sure you're going to cancel the surgery."

She shook her head. "I'm not sure of much of anything, these days." Aside from the fact that she'd ached for him day and night. Ached for him even now.

"Just so you know, I didn't come here to talk you out of anything, Jenna, because it's not my place to do that, or Avery's. But I did come here to read you something."

"Excuse me?"

"It's a letter your father should have given you a long time ago."

He'd done nothing to this point to lessen her confusion. "I don't understand."

"It's from your biological mother."

When Jenna realized that he was about to provide a piece to the puzzle of her past, she ran the emotional gamut—anger, shock, sadness.

Perhaps even fear. But she had to know what she'd yearned to know for years. "Go ahead. I'm listening."

"Dear, baby girl,

Today, I'm going to do the hardest thing I've ever done. I'm going to give you to strangers. I can't keep you because I'm only seventeen and I don't have a job. Your dad is a nice boy, but he went back to his home to Kansas. I can't go home because I've never really had one.

I hear your new parents have a lot of money. That's good, but I hope they give you a lot of love since that's the most important thing. I know because I've never really had that, either…"

Logan paused to clear his throat, letting Jenna know he wasn't unaffected by the content, either.

"…I also know that every day of my life, I'm going to hate myself for not having the guts to try harder. But I promise I'll think about you all the time and I'll always love you, no matter what.

Please forgive me.
Your real mom,
Carol Anne."

She now had a name to go with the face of a mother she'd only imagined—Carol Anne.

The onslaught of tears prevented Jenna from speaking. Tears for the mother she'd never known, a woman who'd barely been a child when she'd given birth to her. A woman who, for some reason, had never known love.

Logan held her close to his side, providing that much-needed crying shoulder. And as she began to regain some composure, more questions rolled around Jenna's murky mind. "Why now, Logan? Why not ten years ago when I first asked him about her? Or four years ago when I was pregnant with J.D.?"

"Avery didn't want you to know that your biological mother was a child from an abusive family who ran away from several group homes. Her life was a mess, Jenna, until the day she died from a drug overdose, two years after your birth."

Jenna had wrongly believed that she could not suffer any more shock today. "I'll never have the chance to meet her and I have no way of knowing if she had the disease, or if she was only a carrier."

"You do know she didn't give you up because she was blind," Logan said. "You also know that, had she lived, she would have regretted the decision. Do you really want to risk doing the same thing if you let David have full custody of your son?"

Jenna could see quite clearly where this was heading. "None of this changes my situation with J.D., Logan. David can still give him things that I can't."

"He can't love him more than you do, Jenna. And Ginger can't replace you as his mother, even if you're thinking that's what your adopted mother did. The difference is, you never knew your biological mother. J.D. knows you, and I don't care what you say, he hasn't forgotten you. And he won't unless you take yourself out of his life."

It all sounded so logical coming from Logan. "David's the one who's bent on taking me out of his life."

"Then fight him, dammit. Fight for your son."

Logan's adamant tone, along with the prospect of missing more of J.D.'s milestones and years of possible regret, fueled Jenna's determination and prompted a decision she should never have had to make. "You're right. I'm going to fight him on this. I want to be there when my child grows up." Yet she still foresaw one problem. "But let's face it Logan, if it goes to court, he has the best argument—a two-parent home."

"We could give him that."

Her shock meter was now off the scale. "What are you saying?"

He took both her hands into his. "I'm saying I want to marry you."

His proposal was totally outlandish, and so was her urge to say yes. But reason didn't always take precedence when the human heart was involved. "You and I both agree that you don't marry for the sake of a child."

"What if we do it for our sakes?"

"Do we really know each other well enough to jump into matrimony?"

"Look, we were both in long-term relationships that didn't pan out. Commitment might be a crapshoot, but we're not. I know in my gut it's going to work with us."

"How do you know that, Logan? How can you be so sure?"

He sighed. "After my experience with Helena, I'd pretty much given up on marriage. I didn't think I'd ever fall in love, either. But here I am, more than ready to get married and long overdue in telling you that I love you."

He'd said it with such heartfelt sincerity, she almost believed him. "How could you possibly know that when you still know so little about me?"

"I know that you burn toast. I know that your lip quivers when you sleep. I know your politics, where you went to school, what makes you afraid. I know your preference for taking up more than half the bed at night, your taste in food and your love of flowery shower gel. I know what you really, really like when we make love and I also know that you are the most headstrong, independent, sexy woman I've ever known. Do you want me to go on?"

She laughed through a few latent tears. "Please, stop. At times you make me sound as appealing as a rush hour traffic jam."

"But there's still one thing I don't know, Jenna."

She smoothed a hand over his face to discover his expression matched his suddenly somber tone. "What's that?"

"I don't know how you feel about me."

She brushed a kiss across his lips. "I know you're as stubborn as I am and that you're the one who takes up more than half the bed. I know the same little tidbits about your personal history and I know exactly what's going to happen when you make that really low, animal sound while we're making love. I also know that you love and respect your mother, which is saying a lot. More important, I knew I loved you the minute you took off my makeup."

"Oh, yeah?"

"Oh, yeah."

"Then we definitely need to get married so we can fill in any missing gaps."

Now it was Jenna's turn to be serious. "We can't rush into this, Logan."

"I'm not saying we should do it tomorrow, or next month, for that matter."

"Good, because I'd like to wait until after I

have the transplants, so I can see the man I'm marrying."

"You already see more in him than anyone else ever has, Jenna."

They kissed a long time then, seated in the garden where he'd almost kissed her the first time, until the lights had interrupted them. And now the sun was responsible for doing that very thing.

Reluctantly, Jenna pulled back. "This light is—"

"Hurting your eyes. I should've realized that. You need to go into the house, anyway, and pack a bag for our trip."

He was certainly full of surprises. "What trip?"

"The one we're going to take together as soon as you're packed."

"If you don't tell me where we're going, I won't know how to pack. Should I bring my hiking boots?"

"Nope, because we're not going camping and we're not driving, either. We're going on a plane."

Just the word *plane* made her anxious. "I hate to fly, Logan. I have since my vision became so poor. I don't like crowds and those narrow aisles and—"

"We're taking a chartered jet and I'll hold your hand the whole time. It'll just be me, you and the open skies. And a crew of two experienced pilots in the cockpit. It also has a nice fold-out sofa in case we get bored on the way."

Jenna felt a serious bout of boredom coming on. "How do you know all of this about a plane?"

"I'm in the transportation business, babe. And I also own the plane, or half of it, I should say. Your father owns the other half."

Having the two most important men in her life working together again couldn't have pleased Jenna more. "So you and my father have finally made amends?"

"We're getting there."

"Speaking of getting there, exactly where are we going?" She pointed at him. "And don't tell me it's a surprise."

"When Avery gave me the letter, we also looked over the terms of your divorce. According to the joint custody clause, David's several months overdue in giving J.D. back to you, even if you originally agreed that he'd stay until you had the transplants. We're going to see if what David told me is true— that he's a reasonable man—by telling him you're ready to bring J.D. home, surgery or no surgery."

As much as she wanted that, she still had reservations. "What if John David doesn't want to come with us?"

"Look, Jenna, he was impressed with a ship. How do you think he's going to feel about a plane he can fly in anytime he wants? Not to mention what he'll have on that plane."

"A widescreen TV with access to every sport channel known to God and little boys of all ages?"

"His mother."

If Jenna had ever had any doubts over whether Logan honestly loved her, they'd all been dispelled. "You're an amazing man, Logan O'Brien."

"You are one helluva woman, Jenna Fordyce."

She didn't have the words to express how much he meant to her, so she settled for the three that meant the most. "I love you."

"I love you, too. And I only have one small condition I haven't covered. If you don't have the surgery in three months' time, we're going to get married, anyway."

"Why is that?"

"Take my word for it. In my family, three months is a lucky number."

Epilogue

Three months later

For the past five minutes, Jenna could only stare at the man standing next to the banquet table in the hotel ballroom. The beautiful man whom she'd married a few hours ago in her mother's garden, surrounded by family and close friends. The first face she'd seen when she'd undergone the corneal transplants nine weeks before. The second had been her child's, who now happily lived in the house she and Logan had purchased the previous month. A lovely two-story home with a large backyard, many trees and myriad flowers.

Though her vision wasn't perfect, the new contacts allowed Jenna to see clearly enough to recognize her image of Logan hadn't come close to the real thing. His eyes were bluer than the early morning sky she'd always cherished, his hair as black as the night she'd once dreaded before she'd met him. And his smile was the kind that had women struggling to find something funny to say so he would reveal those gorgeous dimples. But she'd learned how to do that with only a special look, and she gave that to him now when he met her gaze.

When he held out his hand to her, she crossed the room, her steps steady as she joined the man she'd grown to love more each passing day.

He wrapped one arm around her and kissed her cheek. "Where've you been?"

"Talking with Kevin who I mistakenly thought was Kieran. I don't know how you tell them apart." After you've been around a while, you'll figure it out. Kieran's the one who'll offer sound advice. Kevin will offer to take you out if you get tired of me."

She elbowed his side. "I'll never get tired of you, and Kevin can't be that bad. In fact, he was very cordial and charming."

Logan looked beyond her and grinned. "And it looks like he's charming your friend Candice. You might want to warn her."

"Candice can take care of herself," Jenna said as

she spotted Dermot at the front of the room, standing on a chair that looked as if it might not hold him. "I believe your father's trying to get everyone's attention."

Logan grinned. "Brace yourself, babe. He's about to toast us."

John David chose that moment to burst through the masses and hurl himself at Jenna's legs. "Can I have more cake, Mama?"

She bent down and rubbed the spot of chocolate from the corner of his mouth, the same chocolate that now dotted the front of his miniature tuxedo and the skirt of her satin wedding gown. Obviously, he'd inherited her tendency to wear his food. "We'll see about that as soon as your Grandpa Dermot gives his toast."

J.D. frowned. "I don't want toast. I want cake."

Logan laughed. "Come here and I'll put you on my shoulders so you can see better, bud."

Without hesitatin, John David complied, demonstrating the solid relationship that had formed between her son and her new husband. Jenna had acknowledged that Logan could never replace David, nor would he try, but he would serve as an integral part of the mix of their blended family.

After Logan hoisted J.D. into position, the new family of three turned toward Dermot who had let go a shrill whistle loud enough to wake every hound in Houston.

After Lucy brought Logan and Jenna their own glasses of champagne, she took her place on Jenna's other side and slid an arm around her waist. "I apologize in advance for anything my husband might say."

Jenna wasn't sure what to expect from Dermot, although, she firmly believed it would be interesting.

"Ladies and gents," Dermot began. "We are gathered here today to welcome a new lassie into our family and a new grandpup, too. And on this blessed occasion, I have a wee bit to say to the happy couple."

"Let's hope this doesn't take all night," Logan muttered, earning him a quelling look from his mother.

Dermot raised his glass to Jenna and Logan. "To my middle boy, Logan. You have honored us by choosing a woman who is not only fair on the outside, but just as fair on the inside. And to lovely Jenny, I am glad you have finally seen in Logan what his family has seen all along—a good man with a strong heart and his da's good taste in women. And I'm especially tickled that you can finally see what a handsome man I am."

Following a spattering of laughter, Dermot tapped his glass again and took on a somber expression. "And now I'll be repeatin' the blessing passed onto me from my Irish forefathers. Jenny, Logan and little Johnny, may you be poor in misfortune, rich in blessings, slow to make enemies and quick to make friends. And may you know nothing but happiness from this day forward."

The crowd shouted "Here, here," and in response to the applause, Dermot took a bow. As the band began to play a romantic ballad, Logan set J.D. back on his feet, gave their champagne glasses to his mother and took Jenna's hand. But before they made it to the dance floor, her father intercepted them.

"I'd like to have this dance with my daughter, Logan, if that's all right with you."

Logan regarded Jenna. "It's fine by me."

Jenna smile at the remembrance of other dances she'd shared with her dad. "Of course, as long as you don't expect me to stand on your feet like I did when I was five."

Avery grinned. "Not with you wearing high heels."

After Logan handed her off, Jenna followed Avery onto the floor and took a moment to survey his face—an endearing face she had missed during her time of darkness but had never forgotten. "You're looking rather dapper tonight, Dad."

He set her back and twirled her around before taking her into his arms. "And you're a vision, Jenna. I wish your mother were here to see what a remarkable woman you've become."

She swallowed hard when she noted the slight tremor in his voice. "I know how much you miss her, Dad. And I know how difficult it's going to be for you now that I'm no longer at home. But I expect you to visit us often."

"I'll be fine sweetheart, as long as I know you're happy."

She couldn't begin to express the depths of her joy. "I am. Logan's a good man and he loves me."

"I know. And I want to apologize…"

She pressed a finger against his lips. "You don't have to apologize for anything. But I want to thank you for being the most incredible father a girl could ever hope for."

He bent and kissed her cheek. "I love you, sweetheart."

"I love you, too, Daddy."

After giving her a long embrace, Avery guided her back to Logan. "Take care of her, son. She's a gift."

"You can count on it, Avery."

When Logan and Jenna returned to the dance floor, he held her closely and whispered, "Are you ready to get out of here?"

She was definitely moving in that direction. "Maybe we should wait a bit longer."

He looked decidedly disappointed. "I'm in a hurry to get you in bed."

"We still have a long drive to Arkansas." Some brides might take exception to a honeymoon camping trip, but not Jenna. She found it fitting to start their new life in a place where they'd laid the groundwork for a solid friendship and the start of an exciting future.

"We're not going to Arkansas tonight," Logan said. "I reserved a room upstairs."

That was her Logan, always full of surprises. "I left my bags in the Hummer."

"You're not going to need any clothes."

"True, but unless you have your luggage, then you're going to have to make a stop at the gift shop or risk getting me pregnant." She smoothed a hand over his lapel. "Or we could just not worry about it and make a baby."

Finally, she'd sufficiently surprised him. "I didn't think—"

"That I wanted to have another child? I changed my mind when the geneticist explained that our children have almost no chance of contracting the disease and neither does J.D. When Logan simply stared at her without responding, she added, "Of course, if you've decided you don't want—"

He kissed her gently and smiled. "I can't think of anything I'd like more than to give you a baby, and J.D. a brother or sister, which he's already mentioned he wanted at least five times. And nothing would make me happier than to give my parents the next grandchild before someone beats us to it."

Jenna nodded toward her right at the couple who'd joined them on the dance floor. "I think Devin and Stacy have already beaten us to it."

Logan glanced at his borther and sister-in-law before returning his attention to her. "Do you know something I don't know?"

She shrugged. "I heard a rumor, but don't repeat it since it's not official yet."

He frowned. "If we'd married right after I'd proposed, you'd be pregnant by now."

"Possibly, but I wouldn't have wanted to miss seeing your face when we exchanged vows." Or finally seeing the love in his eyes that she'd sensed all along. "Now, let's hope these transplants hold up so I can continue to see you and our children."

Logan paused and settled his gaze on hers. "If, God forbid, something happens with the transplants, just remember, I'll be your eyes for however long it takes."

Jenna could trust that he would, and she also trusted that, no matter what the future held, his love would always be a constant. She knew she would never wake up alone again, or go to bed alone again. And she vowed never to lose sight of what mattered most—friendship, family and the love of an exceptional man who held her close, but not so close that she couldn't be herself.

She'd found all of that in Logan O'Brien, and so much more.

* * * * *

THE ROYAL HOUSE OF NIROLI
Always passionate, always proud.

The richest royal family in the world—united by blood and passion, torn apart by deceit and desire.

Nestled in the azure blue of the Mediterranean Sea, the majestic island of Niroli has prospered for centuries. The Fierezza men have worn the crown with passion and pride since ancient times. But now, as the king's health declines and his two sons have been tragically killed, the crown is in jeopardy.

The clock is ticking— A new heir must be found before the king is forced to abdicate. By royal decree the internationally scattered members of the Fierezza family are summoned to claim their destiny. But any person who takes the throne must do so according to The Rules of the Royal House of Niroli. Soon secrets and rivalries emerge as the descendents of this ancient royal line vie for position and power. Only a true Fierezza can become ruler—a person dedicated to their country, their people…and their eternal love!

Each month starting in July 2007,
Harlequin Presents is delighted to bring you
an exciting installment from
THE ROYAL HOUSE OF NIROLI,
in which you can follow the epic search
for the true Nirolian king.
Eight heirs, eight romances, eight fantastic stories!

Here's your chance to enjoy a sneak preview of the first book delivered to you by royal decree….

FIVE minutes later she was standing immobile in front of the study's window, her original purpose of coming in forgotten, as she stared in shocked horror at the envelope she was holding. Waves of heat followed by icy chill surged through her body. She could hardly see the address now through her blurred vision, but the crest on its left-hand front corner stood out, its *royal* crest, followed by the address: *HRH Prince Marco of Niroli....*

She didn't hear Marco's key in the apartment door, she didn't even hear him calling out her name. Her shock was so great that nothing could penetrate it. It encased her in a kind of bubble, which only concentrated the torment of what she was suffering and branded it on her brain so that it could never be forgotten. It was only finally pierced by the sudden opening of the study door as Marco walked in.

"Welcome home, *Your Highness*. I suppose I ought to curtsy." She waited, praying that he would laugh and tell her that she had got it all wrong, that the envelope she was holding, addressing him as Prince Marco of Niroli, was some silly mistake. But like a tiny candle flame shivering vulnerably in the dark, her hope trembled fearfully. And then the look in Marco's eyes extinguished it as cruelly as a hand placed callously over a dying person's face to stem their last breath.

"Give that to me," he demanded, taking the envelope from her.

"It's too late, Marco," Emily told him brokenly. "I know the truth now…" She dug her teeth in her lower lip to try to force back her own pain.

"You had no right to go through my desk," Marco shot back at her furiously, full of loathing at being caught off guard and forced into a position in which he was in the wrong, making him determined to find something he could accuse Emily of. "I trusted you…."

Emily could hardly believe what she was hearing. "No, you didn't trust me, Marco, and you didn't trust me because you knew that I couldn't trust you. And you knew that because you're a liar, and liars don't trust people because they know that they themselves cannot be trusted." She not only felt sick, she also felt as though she could hardly breathe. "You are Prince Marco of Niroli… How could you not tell me who you are and still live with me as intimately as we have lived together?" she demanded brokenly.

"Stop being so ridiculously dramatic," Marco demanded fiercely. "You are making too much of the situation."

"*Too much?*" Emily almost screamed the words at him. "When were you going to tell me, Marco? Perhaps you just planned to walk away without telling me anything? After all, what do my feelings matter to you?"

"Of course they matter." Marco stopped her sharply. "And it was in part to protect them, and you, that I decided not to inform you when my grandfather first announced that he intended to step down from the throne and hand it on to me."

"To protect me?" Emily nearly choked on her fury. "Hand on the throne? No wonder you told me when you first took me to bed that all you wanted was sex. You *knew* that was the only kind of relationship there could ever be between us! You *knew* that one day you would be Niroli's king. No doubt you are expected to marry a princess. Is she picked out for you already, your *royal* bride?"

* * * * *

Look for
THE FUTURE KING'S PREGNANT MISTRESS
by Penny Jordan in July 2007,
from Harlequin Presents,
available wherever books are sold.

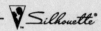

SPECIAL EDITION™

**Look for six new
MONTANA MAVERICKS
stories, beginning in July with**

THE MAN WHO HAD EVERYTHING

by *CHRISTINE RIMMER*

When Grant Clifton decided to sell the
family ranch, he knew it would devastate
Stephanie Julen, the caretaker who'd always been
like a little sister to him. He wanted a new start,
but how could he tell her that she and her mother
would have to leave...especially now that he was
head over heels in love with her?

MONTANA MAVERICKS

Dreaming big—and winning hearts—in Big Sky Country

Silhouette®

Romantic
SUSPENSE

Sparked by Danger,
Fueled by Passion.

Mission: Impassioned

A brand-new miniseries begins with

My Spy

By *USA TODAY* bestselling author

Marie Ferrarella

She had to trust him with her life....
It was the most daring mission of Joshua Lazlo's
career: rescuing the prime minister of England's
daughter from a gang of cold-blooded kidnappers.
But nothing prepared the shadowy secret agent
for a fiery woman whose touch ignited something
far more dangerous.

My Spy
#1472
Available July 2007 wherever you buy books!

nocturne™

**DON'T MISS THE RIVETING CONCLUSION
TO THE RAINTREE TRILOGY**

RAINTREE: SANCTUARY

by *New York Times* bestselling author

BEVERLY
BARTON

Mercy, guardian of the Raintree
homeplace, takes a stand against
the Ansara wizards to battle for
the Clan's future.

*On sale July,
wherever books are sold.*

REQUEST YOUR FREE BOOKS!
2 FREE NOVELS PLUS 2 FREE GIFTS!

SPECIAL EDITION®
Life, Love and Family!

YES! Please send me 2 FREE Silhouette Special Edition® novels and my 2 FREE gifts. After receiving them, if I don't wish to receive any more books, I can return the shipping statement marked "cancel." If I don't cancel, I will receive 6 brand-new novels every month and be billed just $4.24 per book in the U.S., or $4.99 per book in Canada, plus 25¢ shipping and handling per book and applicable taxes, if any*. That's a savings of at least 15% off the cover price! I understand that accepting the 2 free books and gifts places me under no obligation to buy anything. I can always return a shipment and cancel at any time. Even if I never buy another book from Silhouette, the two free books and gifts are mine to keep forever.

235 SDN EEYU   335 SDN EEY6

Name	(PLEASE PRINT)

Address		Apt.

City	State/Prov.	Zip/Postal Code

Signature (if under 18, a parent or guardian must sign)

Mail to the **Silhouette Reader Service™:**
IN U.S.A.: P.O. Box 1867, Buffalo, NY 14240-1867
IN CANADA: P.O. Box 609, Fort Erie, Ontario L2A 5X3

Not valid to current Silhouette Special Edition subscribers.

Want to try two free books from another line?
Call 1-800-873-8635 or visit www.morefreebooks.com.

* Terms and prices subject to change without notice. NY residents add applicable sales tax. Canadian residents will be charged applicable provincial taxes and GST. This offer is limited to one order per household. All orders subject to approval. Credit or debit balances in a customer's account(s) may be offset by any other outstanding balance owed by or to the customer. Please allow 4 to 6 weeks for delivery.

Your Privacy: Silhouette is committed to protecting your privacy. Our Privacy Policy is available online at www.eHarlequin.com or upon request from the Reader Service. From time to time we make our lists of customers available to reputable firms who may have a product or service of interest to you. If you would prefer we not share your name and address, please check here. ☐

SSE07

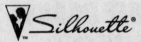

COMING NEXT MONTH

SSECNM0